08/21

The Apple Tart of Hope

'This novel . . . has hidden powers'   *Daily Telegraph*

'Young readers will be hooked from the get-go'   *People*

'A moving and poignant tale about the redemptive
power of friendship'   Louise O'Neill

A Very Good Chance

'A life-affirming read about friendship across a social
divide'   *Sunday Independent*

'Beautifully handled . . . brave and thoughtful . . .
It deserves a wide readership and
confirms Moore Fitzgerald's place as one of
Ireland's most interesting new children's
writers'   *Irish Independent*

Back To Blackbrick

'A tear-jerker with lessons in how to live life
to the full'   *The Sunday Times*

The List of Real Things

'Completely beguiling, and funny
and tender and wise'   Piers Torday

A Strange Kind of Brave

'Gr . . . O'Neill

Also by Sarah Moore Fitzgerald

apping . . . with an incredible twist'   Louise O'Neill

'All kinds of wonderful'   Kit de Waal

ALL THE MONEY IN THE WORLD

SARAH MOORE FITZGERALD

Orion

ORION CHILDREN'S BOOKS

First published in Great Britain in 2021 by Hodder & Stoughton

1 3 5 7 9 10 8 6 4 2

Text copyright © Sarah Moore Fitzgerald, 2021

The moral right of the author has been asserted.

All characters and events in this publication, other than those clearly
in the public domain, are fictitious and any resemblance to
real persons, living or dead, is purely coincidental.

All rights reserved.
No part of this publication may be reproduced, stored in
a retrieval system, or transmitted, in any form or by any means, without
the prior permission in writing of the publisher, nor be otherwise circulated
in any form of binding or cover other than that in which it is published and
without a similar condition including this condition being
imposed on the subsequent purchaser.

A CIP catalogue record for this book is available from the British Library.

ISBN 978 1 510 10414 3

Typeset in ITC Stone Serif Std by Jouve (UK), Milton Keynes
Printed and bound in Great Britain by Clays Ltd, Elcograf S.p.A.

The paper and board used in this book
are made from wood from responsible sources.

MIX
Paper from
responsible sources
FSC® C104740

Orion Children's Books

An imprint of
Hachette Children's Group
Part of Hodder & Stoughton Limited
Carmelite House
50 Victoria Embankment
London EC4Y 0DZ

An Hachette UK Company
www.hachette.co.uk
www.hachettechildrens.co.uk

To Eoghan, Stef and Gabbie; and in memory
of my aunt, Ann O'Dea, for all her music,
and all her magic and all her joy.

CHAPTER 1

A few years ago when Matt, Kitty and I were kids, I got stuck in Violet Fitzsimons's garden. It had been a still evening in late spring and already the air had sweet hints of summer. In the back yard of The Flats, we had spent hours, huddled together, working on our plan. By the time I climbed over the wall and jumped down into that strange, unknown place next door, it had grown dark. And when I realised that I might not be able to get back, I started to feel a bit frightened. But I didn't grasp the full seriousness of the situation until Kitty began to scream.

The early part of the plan had gone quite well.

'You're going to need a torch,' whispered Matt at the beginning of the evening, when we were getting ready for our mission.

'Where will we get one of those?' asked Kitty, running to keep up across the cracked ground.

'Will you two relax?' I said. 'Look, I've got my gloves, and my phone for light, and my backpack for carrying.' I checked my equipment, and lifted the bag over my shoulder.

'What do you need gloves for?'

'Kitty, be quiet,' I answered.

'Why?' she asked.

'Because that's actually the most important part of this entire plan.'

'What is?'

'Being quiet.'

'Oh,' said Kitty, and she and Matt nodded all wise and serious, as if they'd never dream of being anything else.

The night before, Matt and Kitty had been playing around in the back with Kitty's new Frisbee. Matt was the one who'd spun it in the air in the completely wrong direction, which is why it ended up going over the wall. He hadn't done it on purpose or anything. It's just he sometimes had an accidental awkward way about him.

From the expression on Kitty's face we'd known immediately we were going to have to get it back. It wasn't that she cared too badly about the Frisbee. It was just that her mother was easy to annoy, especially when it came to anything new getting lost.

They reckoned it was going to be no problem, which was easy for them to say, since I was the idiot who was going over the wall after it.

'You're the lightest of the three of us,' Matt explained.

'What's that got to do with anything?' I asked.

'And the calmest,' said Kitty.

The plan was this: I was going to climb on to Matt's shoulders, and he was going to push me up, and from there I would jump down easily and retrieve the Frisbee with a swiftness and stealth that apparently only I was capable of.

'But how will I get back?'

Kitty and Matt's faces looked at me all blank.

I made us do some searching among the rubble and the old rusty paint tins in the junk room by the back door where we found a length of thin blue rope.

'Right, listen,' I told them. 'You'll take this rope and hold one end and then you'll fling the other end over the wall so I can grab on to it. Once I've found the Frisbee, I won't risk trying to throw it over. I'll just put it in my bag. All you two need to do is keep hanging on to the rope from your side, and I'll climb back. Got it?'

'Got it!' said Kitty.

'This mission's highly dangerous,' Matt announced.

'Maybe, but we still have to go through with it,' said Kitty.

3

'OK for you to say,' said Matt. 'You're not taking any of the risk.'

'OK for you to say – you don't have a mother who's going to murder you.'

'Not my fault your mother's got anger issues.'

'Not my fault the Frisbee's in Violet Fitzsimons's garden.'

'Stop it, both of you,' I said. 'It's going to be fine as long as the two of you stop arguing. Kitty's mam will never even know it's been lost. Now let's get on with this before I change my mind.'

'OK, sorry,' Kitty said.

'Just be very careful,' added Matt. 'And watch out for the traps.'

Before this, the closest any of us had ever been to Violet Fitzsimons's property was when we sprinted past her front gate, worried that we might catch even the smallest glimpse of her.

Now Matt was crouching low with his hands flat on the wall between her house and our yard, and Kitty was helping me up on to his back.

I knelt unsteadily. Matt rose to his full height while I stood, wobbling, a foot on each shoulder. He grabbed my ankles for a moment, to steady me. From there I clambered on to the top of the wall.

'Can you see it?' hissed Kitty. I dangled my legs over

into Violet Fitzsimons's side and leaned forward, peering into the night air.

I couldn't see anything. I was going to have to jump down, and just like Matt said, I was going to have to be extremely careful on account of all the mantraps – waiting silently in the darkness to snap shut at the slightest touch.

Squinting into the shadows, I could feel the hugeness of the place – the way my breath echoed, the way the breeze swished around, the weird, complicated tangle of smells I'd only ever had a hint of before: flowers and herbs and onions.

I pushed myself off the wall and jumped.

'Oh Jesus,' said Kitty.

'Be quiet,' I replied, finding my feet, my face brushing against something feathery, a plant maybe, or the branch of a tree.

I felt a tickle in my nose. I gulped back three half-smothered sneezes.

'What's happening, Penny?' asked Kitty.

'Are you choking or what?' asked Matt.

'Have you been caught in one of the traps?' asked Kitty again.

'No, I'm just sneezing,' I tried to explain. My eyes adapted to the darkness a little. I could see the outlines of trees and borders of flowers and patches of grass, and things glinting in the blackness, metal things maybe. No point in panicking. Might as well do what I came here to do. It didn't take long. I spotted Kitty's Frisbee, quite near, a glowing redness half hidden inside a low, glossy bush. There was gravel underfoot. It made a crumbly kind of noise. I walked slowly, looking down at my feet, trying not to think about the menacing things all around.

I picked up the Frisbee, shoved it into my bag and turned towards the wall. The rope appeared just as we had planned, toppling reassuringly over, and dangling comfortingly within reach. I grabbed the end and tugged on it.

'Hold on!' Kitty said, sounding like she was trying to be quiet, but actually being very loud.

'Shut up!' I hissed back.

It turns out the rope was the useless slippery nylon kind. As my hands slid down along it, it burned my palms, sending me back to the cold ground.

'Penny! CAN YOU HEAR US?'

Of course I could hear them.

'Please be quiet, Kitty.'

'DO YOU HAVE THE ROPE?'

'I can't get a proper grip of it.'

This was when Kitty's screams began.

'OH JESUS. OH NO!'

Matt joined in. 'LOOK, PENNY, LOOK!'

'What? Look at what?'

'Up there!'

I looked up at the trees. I looked up at the wall, and then

I turned to the great black shadow of Violet Fitzsimons's house. There in the middle of it – glowing and blurred at the edges – was a rectangle of yellow light.

We had done it. We had woken the exact person it was extremely important we did not wake. She was probably staring down at us right now from that suddenly-brightly-lit window, with her narrow murderous eyes and her horrible meat-hook hands.

I scrabbled then as the full load of my terror set in, and still I couldn't get a grip. Three times I made it halfway up and three times I slid back. My friends grew silent. There was nothing in the air now except my own jagged breathing.

Then there was a small click – a tiny noise that held a warning about what was to come. Another light was on now, this time on the ground floor, and there was the proper haunted sound of creaking.

A hunched, hooded shadow appeared, framed by the doorway. Slowly, the figure began to move towards me.

I plunged my shaking hands into my bag, suddenly remembering my gloves, and groped blindly around until I found them and put them on. I got a better hold on the rope as Violet Fitzsimons's shadowy figure kept getting nearer.

I didn't turn around to look but I could hear a rattly sort of wheeze, very close. I hauled myself along the rope, clawing, scratching, kicking my way up the wall.

7

I made it to the top and leapt down on to the scrubby splintered ground of our yard and rolled over a few times, the way you see in movies.

Kitty and Matt legged it over to me.

I pointed to the wall. 'She's right there,' I mouthed.

I struggled to stand up. And the three of us waited, frozen, and Matt pointed a horrified finger at the rope. It still hung limply over the wall but it was being pulled from the other side, inching upwards, the frayed end jolting and skipping and then flipping at the top as it disappeared.

We looked at each other and ran, over the scrub and stone, along the old path of The Flats' back yard, up the leaning steps, through the back door and along the darkened hallway to Kitty's flat. We lay on the floor outside her door. Matt started to laugh, and then so did I. This time it was Kitty who told us to quiet down.

I pulled off my gloves, took the Frisbee out and handed it to her.

'Hope it was worth it. Thought I was dead,' I panted.

'Did you really see her?' asked Kitty.

'Only her shadow,' I said, shuddering at the memory of it.

'Did you spot any of the mantraps?' asked Matt.

'There were definitely things shining in the garden.'

'That must have been them,' Matt said.

Kitty gave me a high five.

'The best friend anyone could ever have, seriously,' she

said, speaking unusually slowly, putting the emphasis on every second word like she was making a speech.

'Nah, I'm not,' I said.

And then Matt and I headed off and up the stairs.

'Penny, seriously, you are so brave,' he said.

'Not brave,' I shrugged, 'just crazy.'

When I put my key in the lock and pushed my shoulder against the door I could hear my mam's snores buzzing softly in the air. I breathed out. She must have missed it all, which was basically a miracle considering the noise we'd made. I hoped all the other grown-ups in The Flats had missed it too. Unlikely though, I thought, sitting up for a while at the kitchen counter, looking through the window into the back yard where no light shone.

The sound of Violet Fitzsimons wheezing was still rattling in my head when I slipped under my duvet and lay in the dark, staring at the ceiling, waiting for my breath to slow.

'PS, I'm never listening to the two of you ever again,' I texted them.

'You never listen to us anyway,' Matt texted back.

'I'm so glad Violet didn't get you. But, god, my nerves,' Kitty wrote.

'*Your* nerves,' I replied and a peculiar wave crashed over me then, full of the enormity of what we had done. I pulled the covers over me and the next thing the birds were singing and the thin morning light of another wet Saturday was dribbling into my room. Another text bleeped on my phone.

'We in v bad trouble.' It was from Kitty. 'Come to Matt's place asap.'

CHAPTER 2

When Matt's granddad opened the door and saw me there, he smiled widely.

'Ah, Penny, love. How are you?'

There was a tea towel draped over his shoulder. It didn't feel like anyone was in trouble.

'Come on in! You'll have a cup of tea?'

'No thanks, Tony,' I said, looking inquiringly at my two friends who were sitting on the sofa, serious and silent.

'What's the story?' I mouthed, but they said nothing.

'Kitty, Matt, you'll have tea?'

'Love one, Tony,' said Kitty. Matt said nothing, only sank deeper into the sofa like he was trying to disappear altogether.

I remember how Matt's gran, Breda, plunged into the room just then, like someone jumping from a height, and grabbed the tea towel from her husband's shoulder while I squeezed in between my two friends. 'Tea? Tony, for goodness' sake! Don't be offering tea to these gangsters.'

She twisted the tea towel into a thick rope, and glared at us, fierce and frowning.

'Nobody's getting anything.'

'We're being interrogated for a crime,' explained Matt.

'What kind of guttersnipes are you at all?'

A note had been sent to Michael Graves, the caretaker. Breda said it had been hand delivered by Violet Fitzsimons herself, late the night before, and the three of us shuddered at the thought of the Fitzsimons hands and all we'd heard about them. The note had complained about how children from The Flats had trespassed on to her land and how a great deal of noise had been made in the middle of the night.

'It was nine in the evening!' Matt corrected.

'It's my fault, Breda,' said Kitty. 'It was my Frisbee. It went floating over the wall and we had to get it back or the mother would have been raging.'

'And did you not think of knocking on her door like any other half-normal human beings?'

'Gran, come on! Don't be ridiculous,' said Matt, as if explaining an important thing to a very small child. 'This is Violet Fitzsimons we're talking about. No one has ever survived a close-up meeting with her.'

'It was awful,' Kitty elaborated, her chin all puckered and wobbly. 'To tell you the truth we're all a bit traumatised.'

'Traumatised?' said Breda. 'I'll give you traumatised.'

'Seriously, Gran,' said Matt. 'There was a while last night when we thought Penny mightn't make it back at all.'

'And why was it Penny who was sent over? What were the two of you doing while she was risking life and limb?'

'Staying alert and vigilant and ready to act,' said Matt.

'Yes,' nodded Kitty. 'You know, in case Violet grabbed Penny by those meat-hook hands and hauled her away.'

Tony handed me a teacup and Breda glared and tutted but then poured tea for everyone and started passing it around. 'Biscuit, love? Or chocolate bar?'

'Did you get a look at her?' Tony asked me.

'Not properly. Only her shadow coming towards me.'

'No more nonsense talk about Violet Fitzsimons, please,' said Breda.

'Gran. It's not nonsense talk. It's fact. Think about the ugliest person you've ever seen.' Matt paused to let the image sink in. 'Well, old Fitzsimons is ten times uglier.' He rolled his eyes so only the whites were showing and Kitty did a disconnected stare – a trance of private, invisible horror.

'My cousin knows a guy whose sister went into Lavender House garden and never came out again,' she said, still staring. 'People say there's a literal dungeon in that house and the girl is still in there – a prisoner in Fitzsimons's basement.'

Matt's gran blessed herself and looked at Tony. 'What'll we do with them, prowling around at night and screeching like a pack of hyenas?'

She turned back to us. 'These are The Flats. Do you not

13

understand how hard it is to keep a good name around here, how easy it is to lose it?'

And even though none of us answered, we all knew what she meant.

Even then, young as we were, we knew what people thought of The Flats. Whenever we told someone where we lived, their eyes would change shape, or they'd glance at their phones, or hold their bags a bit tighter against their bodies, or look at our shoes and then back up at our faces again with a new expression, or finish the conversation abruptly and rush off as if they'd urgently remembered they were supposed to be somewhere else.

People said The Flats were full of rats, and Michael Graves was an ex-convict, and Violet Fitzsimons next door was a witch.

The Flats were once a big house with massive gardens at the front and at the back. Since then, thin partitions had been put up inside the building to divide it into units and bedsits and apartments, and it was full of dark, sour-green corridors, and all the paint on the walls was caked and pocked and peeling, and the yard at the back grew wild with stringy grass and if there had ever been flowers growing there, they were all dead now.

Me and my mam's flat was small and the water pressure was weak, and there were cracks nobody ever fixed in the windows and in the high ceilings, and the lights in the hallways didn't work, and the rent always had to be paid on time and if it wasn't, Michael Graves would come around and hammer on the door with his fist.

The rat thing was true. A couple of years later, when Mam said I was old enough to do our shopping, I spotted one scurrying along the big stairway when I was bringing up the bags. A few days after that I saw one sprinting, startled, towards the wild yard when I opened the front door.

I once heard Rebecca Allinson at school saying The Flats were full of criminals and bed bugs. She said it in a loud voice by the lockers, in front of all her friends.

I'd never seen evidence of bed bugs. And I don't have access to people's criminal records so I can't comment. But I suppose it wasn't hard to imagine Michael Graves having a dodgy past, what with his thousand-yard stare and his complete indifference to human suffering. Apart from him and Kitty's mam though, most of the adults here were nice and kind and generous to each other, and to us.

The rumours about Violet Fitzsimons stayed in our heads. By the time the three of us had grown older and should have known better, the stories and descriptions had got even worse. She looked like a monster and she was easily a

15

hundred years old, maybe more. She never went outside during daylight hours so it was possible, said the rumours, she was actually a vampire and whether she was or not, her intentions were wicked and foul.

My friends and I still sped up when we passed the front gates of her house. Instead of calming us down or reassuring us that Violet would never come near us, Kitty's mother told us if we didn't do what we were told, Violet Fitzsimons would get us. We hated being treated like babies, but old beliefs take a long time to die.

If we were being too loud out in the back, Kitty's mother would noisily open the window and lean out, her fist a white-knuckled knot, jabbing at us.

'IF I'VE TO COME DOWN TO YOU I SWEAR, I'LL THROW YOU LOT OVER THAT WALL MYSELF!' she'd shout.

It was said Violet went out in the dead of night to check the traps with her monstrous hands, stopping at each one to make sure they were well-oiled, ready to be the mechanical captors of invaders who, once caught, would writhe for hours until they were weak and depleted and unable to call for help, and then she'd pull them inside the house and push them down into the dungeon and they'd never be seen again.

Long after the Frisbee rescue, all one of us had to do was say her name and it would be enough to make us scatter back to our own flats, screaming and diving into our beds. We'd

16

text each other then from under our duvets, with trembling fingers. 'Did anyone see her?' Kitty would write, and the glow of my phone screen would light this small pocket of my frightened world, greening my hands and face.

Before they were called The Flats, they used to be called The Rosemary House Apartments and before then they were just Rosemary House.

Rosemary House used to be exactly the same as Lavender House next door. Two smart, identical mansions standing side by side, built by a rich man, one each for his twin daughters. Matt's grandmother told us Captain Fitzsimons was his name. He had been to every country in the world and then settled here in Blackrock and made a fortune in herbs and honey and fruit farming. I used to scrunch up my eyes and try to imagine what our building had been like back then – how our dark, musty halls and stairs and bile-green walls might once have glittered and shone with clean, buttery light.

Me and my mam's apartment was on the second floor. It used to be one big room, but now it was two bedrooms and a kitchen and a small living area. The exterior wall was thick, cold stone and the newer partitions inside had gaps and draughts around the picture rails up near the ceiling, and rough-edged holes at the skirting boards along the floor.

Ours was called a galley kitchen, named after the

kind of kitchen you find in boats where space is scarce. We chopped and cooked and ate there, and sometimes I did my homework on the counter. Our cooker was white and unsteady with little creases of rust dotted all over it like black pepper. Occasionally the frying pan or saucepans would slide off and fall on to the floor. The kitchen's sash window was painted shut, but it let in a good bit of light, looking out over the west side of the untidy back yard.

My room had enough space for a bed and a locker and I was just about able to open my window. From there I could get a glimpse of Violet Fitzsimons's garden, but the wall between our buildings was high and I couldn't see much. Mam's room was towards the front and had no windows. She preferred it that way.

The hall lights in The Flats had push-button timers – big grubby white plastic knobs inside the front door and at the top of each run of stairs. Mostly they didn't work. Plus the one on the ground floor was cracked. Half of it was gone and there were wires sticking out wrapped up in grey masking tape. Vlad – who was one of our favourite grown-ups – had accidentally bashed the leg of his ladder straight into it. He'd done his best to fix it up and was still searching the internet for a replacement switch, but he couldn't find the right match and there was no one else to ask. Michael the caretaker never took care of anything.

On the ground floor in the corner of the cold hallway was a dented metal door. It was scarred with black blotches and covered in yellow tape. It used to be a lift. None of us was allowed to go near it on account of it being a death trap. We could only use the stairwells, which were almost always dark and would have been hard to navigate unless you knew them off by heart like we did. We knew where the broken steps were. We skipped the gaps without breaking our stride, without even needing to look down.

I think it had been Kitty's idea first, to go exploring, even though Mam always told me never to go down to the lower floor on account of the stairs being damaged and on account of how I would definitely break my neck. Matt was enthusiastic, as he often was about Kitty's proposals. He even brought a torch for what he began to call the 'journey below'.

By the time we climbed down the steps and into the belly of our old building we were positive we were going to find great treasures that would be worth a fortune at the very least. Matt's torchlight slid across the dark, dripping spaces, showing speckled mountains – mouldy sheets covering bulky, uneven shapes. We pulled off the covers and coughed and spluttered in the dusty air and we were excited and full of a weird sort of hope. But the things underneath were not treasures at all. Just a load of broken, filthy stuff. Lampshades and car parts and sacks of cement that the damp had got into and were caked on to the buckled floor.

I remember Matt had picked up an old gardening fork then and pretended it was his hand and said, 'I am Violet Fitzsimons and I am coming to get yoooooooou,' and started chasing us around the place and we screamed as we often did, and ran upstairs again to number twelve, where Matt's gran was frying sausages.

'Settle down,' she said with a smile as we tumbled through the door. 'What's all this high jinks for?'

'I am Violet Fitzsimons and I am coming to get yooooou,' growled Matt again, but in his grandparents' cosy flat those words lost their power to frighten, and everyone just laughed.

I remember how Matt's gran had tutted at us. 'Honestly,' she said. 'The poor woman. Those stupid stories.'

For a long time it never occurred to me that the things people said about Violet Fitzsimons might not actually be true. But as I got older, I started to have doubts. Nothing bad had happened to me the night I'd retrieved Kitty's Frisbee even though Matt and Kitty had said if we woke her, I was sure to be toast. We *had* woken her, but she'd only come out of her house and into the garden to see

20

what was the cause of all the commotion. Not exactly the action of a monster, I began to reckon. Just the kind of thing any grown-up would do. And the note she sent to Michael Graves: no one could really blame her. I mean, OK, we'd only been kids at the time, but for all she knew we could have been vandals or robbers.

Most of what we'd heard about her came from the things Kitty's mother said, but a lot of things Kitty's mother said weren't strictly true, especially if it was late in the evening and she'd been at the sherry.

By the time we'd all left primary school and started in Midgrey secondary, I'd begun to change my mind about Violet, and when I passed her front gates, instead of speeding up, I started to slow down. One day for no particular reason, I stood still and peered into her front garden, wrapping my fingers around the bars of the gate, leaning my forehead against its metal coolness.

The distance between the gate and Violet's front door was long but the light was good that day, and the air was clear. The garden was spangled with bright wildflowers. A fat green candle burned and flickered in a bay window. On the top step leading to the front door, a gold-rimmed saucer glimmered and there was a bench and a golden triangle shape on a table. A white cat appeared from behind the bench and stood, half looking at me, with its nose in the air.

A few mornings later there was a newspaper poking through Violet Fitzsimons's letterbox and later the same day when I stopped again, the white cat was there, weaving majestically in and out of the shrubs and tiptoeing across the gravel path. Big bumblebees hovered jerkily among the flowers. And the newspaper was gone.

Everyone in The Flats could hear everyone else's business on account of the thin walls and the badly insulated ceilings. Matt lived on the same corridor as us, and each morning at six o'clock his gran turned on the radio. Exactly half an hour later, her warm, cheerful voice announced tea was ready.

Next, Matt's granddad would get up with a cough like sand and glue. His gran would scold him for it, like he was doing it on purpose, saying, 'You'll wake the child!' The child she was referring to was Matt, who by now was thirteen and the height of a grown man. Twenty minutes later there'd be creaks and thumps and bangs sounding like someone trying to demolish a large object – but it was actually only Matt, finally getting out of bed.

Kitty's mother shouted at her late at night, her words coming out in slurred, angry streams. She told Kitty she was 'useless' and 'no good', and one particular night we heard her roaring that she wished Kitty had never been born. Sometimes we could hear Kitty answering her mother but we could never hear the exact things she said – only a mumble, like she was trying to sing a gentle song. And normally, after a while, Kitty's mam would calm right down again.

In our own roundabout ways we tried to make up for the insults we'd heard by telling her how great she was, by praising her a lot, by not teasing her as much as we teased each other. I never knew whether our compliments made things worse or better. All Kitty would do was shrug her shoulders and smile and seem a bit embarrassed.

Looking back, I think we should have talked to Kitty about the terrible things her mother said. We shouldn't have ignored it as completely as we did. But we were powerless to do anything about the situation and at the time not talking about it didn't feel like denial or disregard. It felt more like a kind of respect.

CHAPTER 3

Kitty and Matt and I used to have a lot of friends at school, but over the years their numbers decreased and then one day it was obvious we didn't have anyone at Midgrey except each other. People stopped inviting us over and we didn't get to hear about any of the events and parties being organised. 'It's because we intimidate them with our brilliance, we're too cool for them, it makes them nervous,' Matt claimed, but we all knew they weren't the reasons.

The last party we'd been at was Grace Grantham's fourteenth. She had floaty balloons and a brilliant, tall cylinder of a cake with a disc of pink chocolate on the top, crowded with sugar flowers and macarons. Timmy Ward brought her a voucher valid for every shop in Dundrum, and Karina Farley brought her a huge leather bag, and David Mack brought her ear-buds, and all the presents were wrapped in shiny paper and tied with complicated bows

24

and everyone clapped and jumped up and down when she opened them and held them up for people to see properly.

I had knitted her a scarf. When I saw what everyone else brought, I told her I'd forgotten to bring anything. Kitty had actually forgotten, and Matt's present was a framed picture he had taken of Grace without her permission or even her knowledge so he too was having serious doubts about whether he should give it to her. In the end he decided against it. Also Matt's grandparents had sent a bowlful of sausages for him to bring so he produced them quite proudly, but when he did, Grace coldly reminded him she was a vegan and left the bowl in the hall where her dog ate a ton of them and then puked on the carpet.

The dog recovered but still, at school the week after, Grace brushed by us at assembly with three of her friends who all glared wordlessly in our direction. The best way to confront passive aggression is to call it out, so I waited at her locker after double maths. 'Hey Grace, why are you ghosting us? We're still going to bring presents. We haven't forgotten.'

'It's got nothing to do with the presents, Penny,' she explained, swinging open her locker and acting like she was in a hurry. 'I don't care about those kinds of things. I'm not shallow. I don't need a present off you.'

'OK, so why are you ignoring me and staring me down?'

She claimed she wasn't doing either of those things. She said she had no interest in me whatsoever any more.

'Why?' I said, and I could feel a mortifying break in my voice.

'Firstly, I'm only friends with people who are prepared to make an effort. It wouldn't have killed you to give me something, even something small. The week after my birthday is not my birthday, Penny.'

'I thought you said it had nothing to do with the presents.'

But Grace had no interest in the logic or consistency of her argument.

'And also you're the one who should have told Matt not to bring those sausages. You're the one who knows I've been committed to a strict vegan diet since the beginning of February. A proper friend would have remembered that.'

For the record, Grace had never once told me she was a vegan. In fact the last time I'd hung out with her, her dad had given us money and we'd gone to the takeaway on the seafront where she'd had the steak sandwich. I knew there was no point in reminding her. Grace was a shape shifter. When she was in first year, she changed her name to Taylor and made the whole school call her it, including the teachers. It only lasted for three weeks, when Mr Galloway forgot and then so did everyone else. At the beginning of second year her online profile said she was a 'yogini' and this year it said she was the CEO of a Harry Styles fan club. By then, Grace was beyond our reach, and we knew it. I could have made all the effort in the world and it wouldn't have mattered.

A few of her friends arrived and huddled around her as she closed her locker. They all stood looking at me too, as if they were part of an organised plan.

'The trouble with you is you don't have any class, Penny, and neither do your friends. Like, sorry if it sounds mean but it is what it is.' This was her public way of terminating our friendship.

'Please don't stop being my friend, Grace,' I'd said before I realised how pathetic and weak it made me sound. Grace and her friends all had the same smile – tight and cruel. And the only thing I could think of was to turn away and walk off.

Actually, if you looked carefully, you could still see some traces of class in The Flats from a long time ago – like the row of bells in the dripping basement. They still gleamed behind a black-edged glass display case on the wall. They used to be for servants, Matt told me. They were connected to the rooms upstairs and depending on which one rang, the servants waiting below would know where they were needed. In my room, there was a little round porcelain handle with a brass circle at the bottom, which was connected to the bell-ringing system. When I first noticed it, it was covered in many layers of paint and I had to gouge around it with my compass until I was able to pull it. I sent Kitty down to the basement and asked her to report back and see if the bells still worked. Kitty made a video of the little bell juddering away and we were both thrilled. Our Flats might have been crap and leaky and broken, but little scraps of old grandness were all around if only you looked out for them.

In the basement there were also candlesticks and torn, framed pictures and great copper dishes and old broken bicycles and tennis rackets with the mesh snapped and curling, and shoes, battered but made of leather and hand-stitched, and empty wine bottles, and big warped books with their pages fused together by damp so no one could read them any more, and boxes full of files.

Matt's gran told me the front door of The Flats was once spectacular and that long ago the downstairs hallway – instead of the dark cave it was now – would have twinkled with thousands of splinters of golden light from a massive chandelier that once hung there. There was nothing like that any more, just flickering blue strip lights hooked up to a timer. Even when they did work they went out much sooner than I could make it upstairs.

I used to sprint up the dark stairs, never having to feel my way along the wall or turn on a torch the way most people had to. It made me feel powerful and strong. It might have been a broken-down old place, but it was our place, and we had the run of it, and we were sort of proud of it I guess – its history and its bigness.

I stopped feeling strong or proud about anything after

Grace rejected me in front of all her friends. Her words began to bounce around my head like hyperactive metal pellets in a pinball machine. *The trouble with you is you don't have any class.*

It wouldn't have hurt so much if it hadn't been true.

Now Grace had pointed it out in public, it began to torment me and erode the things that used to make me happy – taking all my certainties away. All my bravery.

The black patch on my wall started out looking like a tiny mouse, with a pointed nose and a stringy tail. But it ended up looking like an enormous map of Ireland. Mam never came into my room any more and I argued with myself about whether to tell her. She was often unpredictable about stuff like that. If I did tell her, maybe she'd nosedive into one of her silent, gloomy moods. She might say I was somehow to blame. You could never be sure.

For a long time, I decided to say nothing, but eventually it would have been weird not to mention it, considering how big it had grown.

'Mam, there's a stain on the wall in my room, quite big,' I'd said carefully, looking at her from my end of the kitchen counter.

'Oh yes,' she said, light and airy. 'I know all about that.'

'What?'

'I've seen it.'

'Have you seen it's now like a huge map of Ireland?'

She nodded. 'You should make the most of it – to learn your rivers and your counties and your provinces.'

I'd forgotten Mam's other occasional reaction – this strange, random ability to see the stupidly bright side of things.

I entered into the spirit of her suggestion for a while, using the white eraser on the back of my pencil to drag lines across the stain in the shape of the Shannon, Lough Derg, the Barrow, the Corrib. But within a couple of days, the marks were gone, filled in again by the growing blackness, and the stain was bigger than ever.

I googled 'black stain on bedroom wall' and found disturbing things like how it can lead to depression and lung disease and other badnesses. And I remembered about Tony's awful cough and how – from what I could hear through the walls – it seemed to be getting worse.

'We should probably ask Michael to look at it,' I suggested and Mam said, 'Yeah, fat lot of good that will do.'

I tried to cover up the stain myself with tin foil and Sellotape, but the Sellotape didn't stick properly and after a short while, the foil just slid off the wall. I wanted to open the window every night to let fresh air in but Mam said it was much too dangerous, in case of rats.

'Mam, we're on the second floor.'

'Rats can climb up vertical walls in the blink of an eye.

They love it. It's their traditional way of getting indoors,' she replied, looking as worried as I'd ever seen her.

Grace decided to talk to me again but it was only because my clothes had started to smell funny. Somebody had to point it out to me, she explained. I didn't notice it myself at first. Nose-blindness, Grace called it.

'What's the weird stink?' she said one lunch break. Her nose crinkled. She sniffed the air five or six times then grabbed my arm and shoved her face on to my sleeve.

'Oh. My. Gaaaaaawd. What IS that?' she said, standing back from me like I was contagious.

'I don't know,' I said, sniffing my sleeve.

'Well whatever it is, it's disgusting and you should do something about it. Seriously. It's awful. You smell like a zoo. A wet zoo!' Grace swooned backwards into her chair.

Turns out, I wasn't the only source of it. It was the three of us. Matt and Kitty and me. We all smelled the same, apparently. Damp from The Flats. My black, Ireland-map-shaped mould was just one of the signs. Fungus started growing in the back room – biscuit-coloured, trumpet-shaped mushrooms on the carpet – and the clammy, musty smell was getting into everything.

In a way it was a relief to find out I wasn't the only one with the problem. The damp was spreading through the building, creeping into all the flats, appearing on everyone's walls in different shapes. Vlad's was a ghost in his kitchen, and Kitty's was a cloud in her bathroom. And Matt's was a massive rabbit on the ceiling of his grandparents' living area. Tony tried to paint over it three times, but it kept on coming back.

Soon the smell was in our hair and I came to feel as if it was inside us, in our bones and under our skin, and I clenched my teeth together when the crowds at school gathered to make their pitiless accusations about this thing that was out of our control.

Whole clusters of Midgrey students backed away when they saw us coming. And I think it might have been OK, I mean, I mightn't have felt so bad if it hadn't been for the strange, thin smile Kitty put on – her heartbreakingly weak defence against the vicious taunts.

It was official now. We were outcasts – reeking and rotten.

'Rule number one,' said Matt. 'Act like you don't care. Even better, act like you're enjoying the insults. Drives them crazy.'

But I could not pretend such a thing, even if Matt was able to, and even though Kitty bravely did her best. 'Try to imagine we are heroes,' whispered Matt as we walked through the school and crowds parted. 'Like we're astronauts or alien-hunters or crime-fighters. Imagine they're not jeering. Imagine they are the grateful rescued, paying homage to us as we pass in slow motion, set apart from them because of our exceptional brilliance, not our smell.'

Matt's imagination had always been much better than mine.

'Shut up, Matt,' I said.

It was relentless though, and I was not strong. The day Josh Kilmartin and Sadie Green held their noses when they were put near me in class, I just got up and ran out of school. I suppose I'd had enough. I didn't care about what the teachers would say. I didn't care about the trouble I might get into. I didn't think about anything like that. I just skated on my board all the way to Dún Laoghaire pier and stood at the end for ages looking into the snotgreen sea. I wanted to get out of Midgrey and I wanted to get away from The Flats and away from the damp and the rats, and away from not having any class. I wanted a different life, a nicer life. And then I wanted to do a huge dramatic thing, like jump into the water or shout at the sky or at least grab my skateboard and maybe fling it in. But in the end, all I did was sit on the cold granite stone, listening to the squawking of seagulls and the *ding ding ding* of the boat bells. And just as I was picking up my board and getting ready to head home, they came to find me. Two little dots at first, gliding along the pale glowing stone of the long pier, their shapes sharpening and clarifying as they got closer.

'We thought this is where you'd be,' smiled Kitty, and Matt ruffled my hair. He pulled three choc-ices out of his bag and handed one to me and one to Kitty.

'Cool,' I said. I wanted to say, *Thanks a million, Matt.* I wanted to tell them how grateful I was to have friends like them. But if I did, I might cry, and I might not stop for ages and everyone would feel awkward, so I said nothing. The three of us sat above the foamy water, munching away.

'Am I in trouble?' I asked, eventually.

'Don't think so,' said Kitty.

'Galloway didn't even notice you were gone.'

Story of my life.

It was lovely to have friends like them but still the muggy grey humiliation of the day hung over me. When we got home, I didn't feel like going inside.

'Aren't you coming?' asked Kitty. I told her I needed a bit more fresh air and Matt gave me his sweet look with his round, understanding eyes and did a little wave. I sat on the step for a while, then wandered around kicking at daisy heads, and I don't know quite what drew me there, but next thing I was walking over towards Violet's gate. I stood looking in, running my fingers along the black-coiled wrought iron and around the curved handle. Again the candle had been lit, its flame dancing in the bay window. The gold-rimmed milk saucer was there, twinkling on the step.

There was a round stone-edged pond I hadn't noticed before, with flat green leaves crowding the surface. There were rosebushes and white foxgloves and somehow the marble bench looked cleaner, bluer. The triangle on the square stone table was a sundial, I realised. Then I noticed it: the window where the green candle flickered. It was open. And this was when I heard the music.

At first it was so faint, it might have been my phone, or my imagination. I took off my jumper and tied it round my waist, then rolled up my shirtsleeves and wiped my forehead with the back of my hand. I narrowed my eyes and peered towards the window and the flame.

The panes of glass in Lavender House were slightly misshapen and they seemed to ripple in the afternoon sun.

Definitely music. Definitely coming from inside. It got louder and then louder again and soon it was floating, soaring – sweet and mellow and dark and rich and then light and high and bright and clean and brilliant – a gorgeous complication of sound. Sound like I had never heard.

In the unexpected heat of the afternoon, the music untangled me, straightened me out, made my breathing deep and smooth. Without really thinking, I opened the black coil-topped gate and walked in. I sat on the bench, the coldness of the marble seeping into me, cooling me down. I closed my eyes.

Something blinked inside me, like a light going on for the first time. I cupped my hands, palms up, as if the music was liquid falling down on top of me in a silvery wave and I might be able to catch it and bring it home. I don't know how long I stayed listening, but all the time the gorgeous sound swelled in the heat of the afternoon and seemed to find the dark gaps inside me and fill them up. I couldn't explain the feeling. A sort of trance, I suppose you could call it. Maybe it wouldn't happen to everyone. But it definitely happened to me.

The music grew louder again, like thunder.

What am I doing? I thought suddenly, coming out of my strange daze. *Violet might see me.*

I stood and backed out, shutting the gate with a massive clang.

The music stopped and I ran back to The Flats, grabbing my board which I'd abandoned at the front, and rushed through the door, sprinting upstairs three steps at a time.

Kitty and Matt were sitting at the top of the first floor. I nearly crashed into them.

'What's up?' they said together.

'Nothing. Can't stop.'

I dashed past them.

'Come down later for Fifa,' Kitty shouted up after me.

'Yeah, OK, I might,' I shouted back.

All the breakfast stuff was still on the counter but I felt too enchanted and too strange to start doing something as ordinary as the washing-up, so I went to my room and lay on my bed. I tried to silence this new feeling in me that rose above all the other things I'd ever felt.

CHAPTER 4

An internet search of Lavender House revealed it was not famous for mantraps or dungeons or witchcraft or any other monstrous things. It used to be famous for honey, like Breda had said.

There used to be beehives and the honey there had the flavour of lavender, obviously, but other flavours too, like elderflower, orange blossom, blackberry, heather, sage, clover, even firewood. You can buy 'Fitzsimons's Famous Lavender House Honey' in small, stout glass pots. It's got its own website. On the labels it says it has 'curative properties'.

If the article on the internet was true, the brand name was bought out by a huge corporation in 1999 for twenty-two million euros.

There might still be beehives at the back of Lavender House somewhere, I thought. But it was hard to tell on account of how Lavender House held its history close to itself and, I began to realise, was still splendid and complete compared to this creaking, dripping, tumbledown brick twin next door. I thought about the days when the two houses would have been exactly the same – before Violet's had aged with elegance and dignity and ours had become so dark and broken up.

Mantraps have been illegal in this country since 1829 and if they really had been in Violet Fitzsimons's garden, somebody would have seen them and reported them and they'd have been taken away.

It was impossible to uncover any bad stories about Violet anywhere online. I found black-and-white photos of her from long ago and all they did was show how tall she was and how elegant, and that she had a brilliant smile.

Nobody's cousin had disappeared from around here. If a girl *had* actually disappeared, there'd have been missing person reports all over the internet and the name of Lavender House would have been broadcast everywhere and it would have been given a nickname like 'House of Horror' or something similar. And someone would have gone in looking for the girl and there would have been a siege or a search or a forced entry and news headlines about it. But there wasn't anything like that.

Even after you stop believing in a frightening thing, the fear can still echo inside you for a long time, powerful enough to widen your eyes and clench your heart and freeze your body. Fears planted in your brain when you were a kid have been lodged deeply at a time when your brain was soft and malleable, and even when logic kicks in, their old shivering ghosts can remain. Logic is a weak defence.

In my dreams Violet used to have massive steel-tipped boots with pointed teeth and a rasping voice and red veins in the whites of her staring eyes.

But since I heard the music coming out of her open window, and since I found out the only thing Lavender House was famous for was sweet, healing honey, my dreams had started to change. I couldn't stop thinking about how the music had poured out of the window and spilled all over me. In my head I could still hear it.

I was going to banish the mean stories about Violet from my mind and I told Matt and Kitty they should do the same.

'I don't believe anyone who plays music as beautiful as that could possibly be a monster,' I told them.

Mam cleaned offices at night time. I asked her what it was like, wiping off other people's coffee stains and hoovering up the remains of their sandwiches, not to mention the toilets. She said she didn't mind it at all. It was nice, she reckoned, being in a building in the dark and stillness. There was peace in it, she said, but also a sort of interesting rhythm left by the people who worked there, a kind of throb of the day's energy buzzing around the place.

It was my job to wake her when I got back from school so she'd be ready for her shift in plenty of time.

Some afternoons I'd come in and she'd be up, her sheets freshly rumpled. One day, towards the end of the summer term, I turned the corner into the kitchen and she was sitting at the counter sipping tea and staring out into the back yard. She looked at me with bad-news eyes and a trembling chin.

'Penny. Thank goodness you're here. I haven't been able to move.'

'Why not?'

'Rat,' she said, pointing towards the garden. 'I've seen one with my own eyes. I've thought it for a long time, but now I know. There's a rat out there.'

I went over to the window, pressed my face against the glass.

'Where, Mam? I can't see anything.'

'Down by the steps. It hopped into the bushes. I'm sure it's those sacks on top of the skip. Who knows what's in them. And I've been hearing scratching and scrabbling in the walls these last few nights and now I know for sure what's causing it, I'm going to lose my mind.'

The rats had been around for longer than Mam realised.

I'd never told her about the ones I'd seen in the hallway and on the stairs, nor the ones I'd seen rushing out into the

41

back sometimes when I opened The Flats' front door. She did not take this sort of news well.

'Don't worry too much about it, Mam. Maybe it was a field mouse. They're harmless.'

'Penny, listen, listen to me,' she said, her eyes getting glossier, her hands clinging together. 'It was a rat. Dark. Grey. Big as a guinea pig. Bubonic.'

'Mam, the bubonic plague died out in 1750.'

'OK then, what about Weil's disease, Lyme disease, typhus? Action needs to be taken.'

'We could talk to Michael about it.'

'He never does anything.'

'I could say it to Matt's granddad?'

'Oh yes, good idea. Tell Tony. He'll know what to do. That would be great because I have to leave early for my shift. The car's banjaxed.'

'What do you mean?'

'It's not working. It's got steam rising from the engine and now it won't start. Don't know how much that's going to cost.'

Mam bit her lip and looked at her watch.

'Right then, I'll tell him,' I said. 'But how are you going to get to work?'

'I'll get a taxi. I can use what's in the money jar.'

Mam tried to smile a little bit.

'Do you need me to get anything from the shop later?'

'No,' she said, staring back out through the glass.

42

I swung the fridge door open. 'Mam, there's nothing in here. We need milk. We need butter.'

My phone bleeped.

'Call ovr pls. We need u 2 help with something.' It was Kitty.

Mam got up and put both her hands on the rim of the sink like she was steadying herself against a terrible thing. She pressed her lips together and took a massive breath like she was trying to suck all the air out of the room.

'Right, well if I'm going to be on time I'll need to leave this minute.'

'Is that enough money for a taxi?' I said, glancing at the jar.

'Well if it's not, I'll have to figure that out for myself, won't I?' she said, stuffing her apron into her bag. 'Just like I have to figure everything out.'

She brushed past me and grabbed the jar, peering into it.

'So forget about the milk. Forget about the butter. I need this. Payday's tomorrow. We'll just have to wait for milk and butter till then.'

'But what's there to eat?' I asked.

'There's a slice of bread left and a tin of beans. Make do. I've got to go.'

She didn't even say goodbye. Just slammed the door, harder than she needed to, and I sat with my elbows on the counter waiting for her footsteps to fade. I wandered around the flat then for a while feeling angry and wrong-footed. I went to my room, sat in my chair, stared at my wall, where the stain was starting to look like the whole of Europe.

'COME ON PEN! WHERE ARE U?' came Kitty's next text.

By the time I arrived at Kitty's, she was pulling two books out from under the table.

'No. No way, not again,' I said, backing away.

'Pen, come on. Please. It's only going to take you a second.'

Matt was digging for his books too.

'Seriously. Guys. You haven't even started?'

'But we hate it and you love it so much. It's more like us doing you the favour.'

'Yeah right,' I said.

'Please, please, please,' said Kitty.

'We'll do anything for you,' said Matt.

'OK then,' I said, noticing how hungry I suddenly felt. 'How about one of your gran's sausage sandwiches?'

'Ooh, I dunno about that, it's very late notice,' said Matt, but Kitty gave him a look and then Matt texted his gran and we all sat around waiting until Matt's phone beeped back.

'I do believe we've got ourselves a deal!' he said, and the two of them cheered and we raced out of Kitty's and up to the second floor where Breda was standing at the door.

'Sure I'm only delighted,' she said.

'She lives to feed people,' explained Kitty in a whisper. 'It's basically her whole purpose in life.'

It felt wrong doing other people's homework, I suppose, but part of me didn't really mind. So I plonked myself in front of Matt's grandparents' blaring TV with everyone chatting in the background. It didn't take me too long and the sandwich was delicious, all soft fresh bread and loads of butter and crispy sausage sliced up evenly.

'This is the last time I'm bailing you two out,' I told them as I handed the copies back, and they said, 'Thanks, Penny, you're a superstar.'

There were lots of days when Kitty didn't go to school at all and when she did, she was failing everything, even things nobody fails, like CSPE. Matt wasn't much better. His grandparents were extremely proud of his attendance record, but the truth was he was barely keeping up either.

I was the only one from The Flats who was getting good grades but I was an outlier, an anomaly. No one in the history of Midgrey School got the grades I got.

The following Saturday morning was hot and I'd slept badly. I woke and wandered into the kitchen. I always loved the weekend after payday because we'd have done the shopping by then and there would be plenty in the fridge. As I turned on the tap there was the miserable whine from the pipes that meant the water was off. All the glasses we owned were dirty and piled in the sink.

Groggily, I stared out through the kitchen window. A bright splodge of whiteness shone out against our grey scrub background. It was Violet Fitzsimons's cat. If she was a human, she'd have been a celebrity, like Angelia Jolie or the lead singer in an opera. She held her tail upright as if trying to keep herself as high above the ground as she could, as if she knew this place was beneath her dignity.

I put some toast on, drank a glug of orange juice from the carton and continued to watch the cat from the window. She could see something I could not. She was crouching low down, perfectly still, except for her twitching tail and her ears, two furry periscopes, swivelling. The toast popped and I went to grab it. When I looked down at the garden again, Violet's cat was gone.

Later, when the water pipes finally came back on and the sink was hot and soapy, and I was dousing our dirty glasses, I heard a terrible noise, rising up through the building from far below. It was my mother, wailing my name. I fled down the stairs past open doors with faces peering out. 'It's OK, I'm coming, Mam,' I shouted, not letting myself think about what catastrophe was down there. 'Hold on!'

Mam was standing in the dark hall, her whole body shaking, and it seemed like she was smudged at her edges, like she was surrounded by a strange mist. She was pointing at the floor.

At first I thought she was pointing at a fat grey purse slumped on the doormat. But it was not a purse. It was a rat. Dead.

'Vermin, inside now. God almighty, I knew it. Did you not tell Tony?'

'I forgot,' I admitted.

'Christ almighty, Penny. We could all be dead with disease in this place before anyone would do anything about it.'

Kitty's mother appeared too. She didn't say a word, just walked over to Michael Graves's door and began slapping it with the flat of her hand over and over again. Finally, a creak of yellow light shot into the hallway and Michael wandered out. His hair was messy. His stained, too-small t-shirt was stretched across his belly. He scratched his head.

'Mike, hello Mike,' my mam said, as if they were friends. 'Something needs to be done about this.'

'About what,' he said, yawning.

'About the rats,' we all replied together.

'There are no rats in this building,' he said without looking anyone in the eye.

'Michael, will you please refer to the evidence in front of you,' said my mother, pointing again at the rat.

But Michael's face stayed blank as it always did, and he just blinked.

'It's the cat from next door,' he insisted. 'It goes hunting. Brings the bodies here. The problem is the cat.'

In the end, Matt's grandparents came down to sort it out. With rubber gloves and tutting noises and a black plastic bag, they swept up the rat and threw it away, and Tony said, 'Let's hope it's the last one,' and Breda washed down the whole place with bleach and spray, and the way they did it all so fast and so automatically made me pretty sure they'd done it before.

Matt reckoned that Mike must be the only caretaker on the planet who thought cats were the *cause* of a rat problem.

'I know,' I said, 'and I think he might be planning to actually kill the cat.'

'And then the rats will take over, and everyone in here will have full-blown nervous breakdowns,' said Kitty.

'I don't really know why everyone freaks out so much about them anyway,' said Matt. 'They're clever animals. They're brave. I saw a programme about a rat that got a medal of courage for detecting landmines in Cambodia.'

'Shut up, Matt,' said Kitty. 'Courageous or otherwise, nobody wants them crawling around The Flats.'

Useless as he normally was, it turns out we'd slightly underestimated Michael Graves on the issue of the rodents, because the next day, little piles of crumbly blue pebbles of poison had been placed in the corners of The Flats – along the stairs and by the door and in the yard outside and by the entrance in the front. Signs were written in pale biro on torn, lined paper and pinned up all over the place:

RAT POISON LAID. DO NOT TOUCH OR EAT.

'Makes them mad,' Kitty explained. 'They get parched so they all run off towards the river. Then they'll kill themselves through over-hydration, drowning in their own thirst.'

Matt said he preferred not to think about it.

And soon the scrabbling and scratching in the walls slowed down and by the following weekend it had stopped completely. The relief that trickled around The Flats was like an anaesthetic. For the first time in ages, Mam slept properly. Now that Michael was on a roll I asked her if maybe he could be persuaded to get rid of the huge black patches everywhere, but she didn't seem to care so much about the damp, even though it was now making her cough too and ruining my life and the lives of my friends on account of how we were still being mocked at school for the way we smelled.

The next weekend, Mam's deep, long, untroubled snores woke me up early. I dressed quietly and slipped downstairs to see if one of the others might be around.

That was the morning I found Violet Fitzsimons's white cat, lying stretched out and motionless by the back door.

I crouched down and put my hand on her back. She was warm and breathing still, but there was a thin dribble of blood drawing a line from her mouth to the concrete ground. I slid my hands gently underneath her floppy body. For a second, she jolted in my arms. 'It's OK. I'm taking you home,' I whispered. She seemed to relax a little then, like she knew she could trust me. I walked slowly, afraid I might cause her pain, afraid of where I was going, but calling on my own courage all the same.

'You poor thing. You poor thing,' I kept saying. I shoved my shoulder against the swinging door from the back yard and stepped slowly through our dark hallway. A glint of Mike's yellow light sliced through the air, and he stood in the doorway watching me. He sniffed, and then he spat. I never hated him more.

Look what your cheap solution is doing – killing this beautiful animal who has done nothing wrong, I wanted to say, but Mike's stare was hard and cold, and in the end I said nothing to him, and he said nothing to me.

Out the main door, along the broken flagstones, through our old rusted gates and left towards Violet's black ones. Slowly, with my elbow, I pulled down the handle, and I kicked the gates open. I tried to breathe evenly and calmly as I approached Violet Fitzsimons's door.

CHAPTER 5

The saucer was full right up to its gold-rimmed brim, a layer of wrinkled creamy skin on the top.

The door knocker was dolphin-shaped, huge and heavy. With the cat so fragile in my arms, it was a struggle but I was careful. Lifting the knocker, I made five big bangs and shouted, 'Hello, hello, help, hello!'

I didn't think anyone would come but then a shadow appeared behind the coloured panes of glass, and slowly, the shadow grew larger. My legs felt a bit wobbly but I steadied myself. I could feel the cat's heart beating, or maybe it was mine, or both of ours together. Then the sound of creaking footsteps. Then the click of a lock being unlatched and the groan of the big door opening slightly.

Then, a huge curved knife lunging out of the door, held by a bony hand.

'This is a kukri knife,' said a calm, silky voice, 'which is to say I am holding a Nepalese blade, which could do a great deal of damage. I will not hesitate to use it if you come any nearer. Go away at once.'

'I come in peace,' I shouted, fast and stupid. 'And I come in rescue. Hello, I'm sorry but . . . your cat . . . she's still breathing . . . but it's poison . . . there were rats . . . it was the caretaker . . .' And suddenly Violet Fitzsimons threw open the door.

She was very tall. Her hair was the mystical white of a druid. Her jacket was crushed raspberry velvet and she wore slim black trousers. There were pink silk slippers on her feet. The crooked silver knife dropped from her hand with a clang and skittered on the stone below.

'Oh dear, my goodness,' she said.

'I am so sorry. It wasn't me. I want to help.'

'Hush,' she said. 'Come in,' and then added, 'I was just making dumplings,' as if this was somehow relevant.

I stepped over the threshold and stood in the old golden-aired hallway. In some ghostly way, it felt a little as if I was standing in the hallway to our Flats – all the same proportions, except in every other way it was different here: rich and light, and flooded with colours coming through the glass in the door and through a stained-window skylight, high above, which made dappled splashes of blue and yellow and green on the floor and on the furniture and on the walls. Gently, Violet disentangled the cat from my arms and lowered herself on to a tapestry chair, arranging the cat on her lap with great care, and lifting an old, heavy black phone.

'Hello, dear Jeremy, could you come now?' she said and I was glad she'd got an answer so quickly. 'I'm afraid it's rather urgent. It's dear Bluebell. She has been poisoned.' Violet glanced at me again with an expression I could not read.

'Perhaps it is already too late, but do come please, straight away. Fast as you can.'

There was a steadiness in her voice and such directness about her. She was old but she was beautiful and though she was definitely strange, it was in some lovely way that I still cannot describe or explain.

'Please sit,' she said, pointing at an identical chair facing hers, and I was glad to. 'It's simply a matter of waiting for Jeremy now. He is my vet and he will know much the best thing to do. Until then, we must remain calm.'

While we waited, I gazed at her in a way I felt sure must have seemed weird. Her hands were nothing like meat hooks after all. They were lovely. Long pale fingers. Nails the shape of almonds.

'I must apologise. I'm afraid it was awfully impolite of me to brandish a knife earlier, and not to have introduced myself,' she said, as if not introducing herself was at least as rude as waving a knife at a stranger. She stroked Bluebell's back. 'I am Violet Fitzsimons.'

'I know,' I said.

'Gosh, yes I suppose you must or else you wouldn't be here. And thank you very much for this errand of mercy. Who are you?'

'I'm Penny. Penny Nolan.'

'And where are you from, Penny?'

I paused for a second.

'I'm from The Flats. Second floor.'

'Next door?' she said.

'Yes.'

I wasn't surprised by the silence that followed. I was used to this kind of reaction. I waited for her to tell me to leave. But she did not.

'I'm so sorry about what's happened,' I blurted. I could feel my chin quivering then. I put my hands to my face.

'Oh no, dear, now don't be upsetting yourself. It is exceptionally kind of you to have brought Bluebell back to me. And now, if she does die, it won't be in some lonely corner, it will be here with me and that in itself will be such a comfort. To be frank, I did worry this might happen one day. She is a wanderer, you see. You can't keep a free spirit locked up.'

We sat in that golden-lit silence for another while and Violet's elegant hand kept stroking Bluebell's motionless body. There were loads of other things I'd like to have said but I couldn't think of how to begin, and soon Jeremy arrived. A short man in jeans with a green tie under a

V-neck jumper, carrying a rectangular red bag like a Swiss flag over his shoulder.

'Hello, dear boy,' said Violet.

'Hello, Violet,' said Jeremy and the two of them air-kissed each other. He looked down and said, 'Poor old Bluebell. May I?' and lifted the cat into his arms like she was a human baby. 'Can we take her into the kitchen?'

'Yes, of course, do come along,' said Violet.

The kitchen was a cavern of a place. Wet lace and linen squares hung on a long wooden rail up high, attached to a rope and a pulley. The rope was twisted over and over again into a figure of eight, on a brass peg that was screwed to the wall.

Jeremy set up a temporary examination table on the black stone-topped island and the whole time, Violet remained calm. I thought maybe she was in a kind of shock or that she hadn't fully grasped the situation.

'I expect everyone could do with a cup of tea.' There was no plug or flex attached to her kettle. She filled it and walked over to an oven with cream-enamelled doors at the front. She lifted a big lid on the top by its spiral handle, and put the kettle down.

Jeremy took out tubes, a see-through bag of water and a small stand.

'Yes, indeed, it does look like a case of poisoning, but our clever Bloob doesn't seem to have taken too much of it. I think I may be able to flush it out of her system.'

He held a syringe up to the light, a beaded bubble twinkling at the tip, and plunged the needle in. Bluebell seemed to sigh.

'Where's her basket?' he asked.

'Yes, oh, dear Penny, would you do me a great favour? The cat's basket is in the basement, would you mind very much fetching it for me? Just out through the kitchen door and down the stairwell there to the left.'

I said no problem, but when I got to the top of the stairs, I held on to the bannister and paused for a moment. The old stories about Violet's dungeon began to echo up at me like a whisper, and I wondered whether this actually was a trap, and whether there might in fact be a metal cage waiting for me down there after all, ready to bang shut and contain me in some horrifying automatic way, and that the worst of the old fairy-tale terrors would not just be real, but would turn out to be the story of my unfolding life.

I reminded myself I didn't believe in stupid things any more. There was nothing to be afraid of.

And when I got to the bottom there was no cold ground and there were no chains and I could see no cages. Only shell-pink carpet and low, soft light and pictures on the walls, of mountains and waterfalls and sunsets in faraway places.

The basket was right there, just as Violet had said it was, and I collected it into my arms and flew back up again. Across the hall, I glimpsed a half-open door and the shining, glossy black corner of what I already knew must have been Violet Fitzsimons's piano.

Jeremy laid Bluebell carefully into her basket next to the big oven.

'Well now, I'm very relieved to be able to tell you my verdict,' he announced at last. 'There is an excellent chance she is going to make a comprehensive recovery.'

Violet closed her eyes.

'Tremendous news, dear Jay,' she said, opening them again, and her face got softer, and new colour seemed to pour into her cheeks. She invited Jeremy and me to stay on – not only to have a cup of tea but also a bite to eat.

'I've just made some strawberry dumplings,' she said.

'Violet, I'd love to, but perhaps another time. Must dash. Am glad to have been of assistance to our patient. Bluebell should sleep this off and I will come back in the morning to check on her and remove the drip. If she wriggles out of it before then, no need to panic. It will be a good sign. Give her plenty to drink. Any other concerns, you know where I am.'

Violet showed Jeremy to the door, and I stayed with Bluebell who was sprawled out in her basket now, looking like a slightly injured queen.

'You'll be OK,' I whispered, and the tip of her tail trembled slightly.

On the walls of Violet's kitchen were strong shelves full of bottles and flasks and jars, rows and rows of them with labels saying 'flour' and 'sugar' and 'oats' and 'lavender honey' and 'rosemary honey' and 'thyme honey' and 'gooseberry preserve'. Wooden spoons stuck out of blue and white stripy pots. Big chunky-handled copper pans hung from pegs on the wall.

'I am so very grateful to you,' said Violet, who made me jump on account of having come back in so quietly. She emptied the boiling water into a teapot with pale pink flowers on it, and after a few minutes poured tea into two cups and gave one to me.

'Please help yourself to milk or sugar or lemon.'

She squeezed juice from a wedge of lemon into her cup and took a sip.

There were so many things I wanted to say to her then. How lovely she was. How she had such an excellent and interesting kitchen. I wanted to ask her if she knew what people said about her, and if she did, I wanted to tell her I'd never believed any of it. I wanted to ask her if I could go in and touch the piano and I wanted to say how I'd heard her beautiful music. But by then I'd lost my nerve.

Instead I asked her about the honey. She said, 'Why yes, yes, this is the original headquarters of the world-famous Lavender House honey brand. I tried my best for a long time to carry on with it, and I love the thought of how proud it would have made my father, who was a wonderful farmer. But for all sorts of reasons, it was a relief to let the business go in the end. If the truth be known, I was never the farmer of the family. Not the outdoor type. Give me a cup of tea and a piano! They are the things that warm my heart.'

I ended up staying for ages, and I couldn't stop thinking about all the years this lovely woman lived next door to us, and how none of us would go near her on account of us thinking she was a monster. And when I left she said she very much hoped I would come back again any time, and it gave me the courage to call in the next day to see how Bluebell was.

There were lots of photos hanging on the walls of Violet's house – most of them were black-and-white ones of girls in school uniforms. On the crest of the uniforms was an open oyster shell. The faces of the girls were smooth and old-fashioned and they wore ribboned plaits and draped their arms around each other, and in the biggest of the photos a huge lawn spread out in front of a great sprawling castle of a building. I stared at the faces until one seemed clearer than the rest. And I stared at it some more until I realised why it was so familiar.

'Is this you?'

Violet laughed. 'Yes. It is. From terribly long ago. How could you have guessed?'

'Because you look the same,' I said.

'A compliment indeed, dear girl, but sadly untrue.'

And I said, 'No, really. I recognised you straight away. What was the name of your school?'

'Pearlbourne.'

'Pearl what?'

Her eyebrows rose high on her forehead and she held herself even taller, and somehow there was a lightness in her then.

'Pearlbourne. You know. Pearlbourne Academy for Exceptional Girls?'

'I've never heard of a place called that,' I said.

'But you must have,' she replied.

'You look so happy,' I said, staring back at the faces again. 'Did you like it there?'

'Ah, indeed,' she sighed. 'They say it's the tragedy of all Pearlbournians – they may never again be happier than they were at school. Such wonderful days.'

'Really?'

'Oh yes. I hold those years inside me always. They give me strength. It's no embellishment to say Pearlbourne was my foundation. It prepared me for the rest of my life, for the slings and sorrows to follow.'

'Wow,' I said. 'I can't imagine anyone ever being happy at school.'

'What an extraordinary thing to say,' she said. 'Presumably you say it because you are not happy in yours?'

'Miserable. I only go because my mam would hate it if I didn't.'

'Do you struggle with the subjects? Are your teachers harsh and uncompromising?'

'No, it's the opposite. It's the students who are mean. And the teachers, well I guess they're OK, but no one pushes me or asks me to work harder or anything.'

'Gosh, this does sound grim and unusual,' she said.

As Bluebell made her luxurious recovery by stretching and yawning and nibbling on little fragments of smoked salmon fed to her from Violet's gentle hand, we talked about Violet's school days of long ago.

'Literature taught by poets and writers. Ballet led by Madama Magda. Never knew her last name. She'd defected from Budapest, had a terrible limp, walked around us with a stick, often wept while we girls were dancing. Oh, the memories! Ivor McGregor for horse-riding – of the McGregor clan, equestrianism in their blood for generations. And oh, the famous walled maths garden. Deep inside the grounds, in the heart of the Pearlbourne forest, exactly a mile from the front entrance to the school. We had to measure its distances with a clicking roller. It was a magical place, full of delight, and hair-raising trampolines and pulleys and swings and giant compasses and protractors. Wouldn't be allowed now, of course – the world has gone so faint-hearted and spineless. Miss Fortune – our maths teacher, and the happiest person I've ever known – made us calculate the angle of the sun and weighed us and tested probabilities with all manner of experiments. To this day, I cannot do the smallest piece of mental arithmetic without remembering the sensation of whizzing through the air, tied to a rope! Our English teacher, Miss Heaney, was forever having to summon us. She often had to cycle along the forest path and ambush our activities by dashing through the doors in the wall, and clapping her hands beckoning us back out of the forest and up the path and indoors for poetry.

'Ah, Pearlbourne Academy,' Violet whispered then, as if it was a sacred thing. 'It was the very making of me. But most magical of all was the music room! One room full of the very finest pianos all tuned to perfection, a huge window looking out over the Pearlbourne lake – and another one for strings and another for wind instruments and then a concert hall to bring all the sounds together.'

I tried to imagine the young Violet Fitzsimons on a swing in a maths garden measuring the curve of her movements, or playing piano in the music rooms. 'It would be so great if there was still a school like that.'

'Oh, but there is,' she said. 'Pearlbourne is going strong. A vibrant community of teachers and students. Us old girls are invited back there once a year for the annual reunion. I've never been. I'm sure it's all quite changed now, modernised and tarted up and whatnot, and perhaps some of where we learned and played is concreted over, but when I was there – oh, glorious!'

She paused and gazed off to a faraway place, her eyes kind of glossy. And then she sniffed, and looked at me with a slight jump as if for a second she'd forgotten I was even there.

'Dear, dear, I suppose it doesn't do to go back to places where you've been happy once. The nostalgia could quite overtake one. Have you really never heard of it?'

'Never.'

'I imagine these days they must have to be rather private and protective, what with the panopticon of the internet and girls from important families and so on.'

I asked her what panopticon meant.

'A way of keeping people under surveillance without their knowledge or permission.'

I put down my empty teacup and told her I'd better be going. She came with me to the hallway.

'I'm going to make sure they get rid of the poison,' I promised. 'I couldn't stand the thought of anything happening to Bluebell again.'

'Indeed,' Violet replied. 'Poison is such an awful strategy for vermin control. I can't bear how it seems to have become the standard treatment for rat infestations everywhere. But strictly speaking it should be stored in special containers that only rats can enter. Whose idea was it to leave it out in the open for any poor creature to ingest?'

It was Michael Graves's fault, I told her. He hadn't used

containers, only badly-written signs, which cats obviously cannot read.

'No idea why he doesn't just get a couple of cats in himself,' she said. 'So much safer. Much rather the natural law of the jungle than the sinister laws of the pharmacist, don't you think?'

I nodded.

'Oh, I almost forgot, I have something for you, hold tight there a second.'

As she hurried off across the hallway again, I wandered towards her tapestry chair. There were more silver-framed pictures on the shining hall table. I picked one up and looked at it. A much younger Violet, standing in front of a piano, holding a bouquet of flowers.

I heard Violet's steps again and quickly put the picture back. At first I didn't recognise what she was carrying, all wound up in an elegant knot, but then I saw it was our useless nylon rope.

'I've had this for a few years now. Kept meaning to drop by with it but I never got round to it. Thought you might want it back,' she said. 'You can tell your friends: if they ever happen ever to lose anything over my wall again, they are welcome to come to the door. Much safer. I won't eat them! Haha!'

I was mortified but said thank you.

'My dear, the pleasure is all mine. So glad you called

again. It's been a long time since I've had this much company. And two days running! I do hope it means you're turning it into a habit.'

I couldn't stop thinking about her. I didn't sleep properly for three nights.

CHAPTER 6

$\mathbf{M}$am was scraping a knife along the top of the butter making a thin curl. Since the rat scare, she'd developed a strange, watchful way about her. I was doing my homework on the counter. It was going to be butter sandwiches for tea.

'Do you think they'd let someone bring a piano in here?' I asked her, and maybe it was an out-of-the-blue question because she stopped in the middle of a butter curl and just looked at me.

'A piano? Is this a trick question? Some kind of quiz?'

'No. I'm wondering if we might be able to get one. I've got interested in piano recently, Mam, and I think I'd really like to learn how to play.'

'We? As in you and me? Get a piano? And bring it up here?'

Mam's laugh started out softly but gradually her shoulders began to shake and then her laugh grew louder and I said, 'What, Mam, what's so funny?' but she couldn't speak. Tears fell down her cheeks. The edges of her face went purple like a bruise, and she started to cough and had to go and sit down on the low chair and wipe each of her cheeks with a piece of kitchen towel.

'Seriously, Mam, what?'

'Ah ha ha, oh ho.' She sniffed, calming down a little, taking her pack of cigarettes out of her pocket, pulling one out, lighting it and then breathing in heavily, as if she needed a lungful of tar and nicotine to recover from the hilariousness of my request.

'Penny, do you know how much pianos actually cost?'

I didn't know but I checked. Mad expensive, it turns out. 'But I could get a keyboard for about a hundred euros, less even, and that might do for the moment', I suggested the next day.

'Right, fair enough. You'll have to wait for your birthday,' she said but this was only May, and my birthday wasn't until November, and something important had begun to burn inside my heart. There was no way I was going to be able to wait.

Mam's persistent cough was the first noise I heard when she got up and the last thing I heard before she went to bed. She claimed it was because of all the stairs she had to climb on account of the lift being permanently broken. Those stairs would be the death of her, she said. I disagreed. If anything was going to kill her it was the stupid cigarettes she kept smoking. I suggested the stairs might actually save her life since they were the only exercise she got.

'I get plenty of exercise,' she told me. 'Hoovering other people's carpets, scrubbing other people's toilets, shining other people's floors. You think that's not physically strenuous?'

She wished we were on the ground floor like Vlad.

'I pay extra. Is worth it,' he explained one day when I was helping him in with his stuff. 'Heavy equipment. Stairs too many and too much.' Then he laughed his head off as if he'd just said something terrifically funny.

When he'd first arrived at The Flats, Vlad owned a tiny battered car with rust around the wheel rims and a huge scratch gouged into the passenger seat, and sweeping brushes and mops and the ends of ladders sticking out of all the open windows. But he had smartened up a lot since then. Now Vlad's old car belonged to Mam – she'd bought it off him for a 'crazy deal' and Vlad had a van all clean and white and new. On one side was written, CLEANING MAY NOT KILL YOU. On the other, it said, WHY TAKE THE CHANCE? He was forever pointing out his slogan to strangers and laughing his outlandish laugh and people usually ended up laughing with him too. Vlad was infectious like that.

'Thank you, Penny. You very kind girl,' he said as I held the front door open for him. He clattered in with buckets swinging and a stepladder weirdly balanced over his shoulder.

'Hey Vlad, mind if I talk to you for a sec?'

He stopped in the hallway and put all his stuff on the floor.

'Talk to me for a sec? Penny, you can talk to me for a minute, for an hour, whatever time you like!'

'I'm looking for your advice.'

His face darkened a little.

'I do not give advice, it is dangerous,' he said.

'Please, I need to figure out a way to make some money.'

'Ah, I see. OK, that is different. I can help you. Sit.'

I sat on the bottom step beside the wall and he sat on the other side by the bannister.

'You owe money? You in trouble? How much you need?'

'No trouble,' I told him. 'I just want to buy something.'

Vlad raised one thick eyebrow, then the other.

Ever since I'd heard Violet's piano, the ache hadn't gone away. Violet's music had woken me up. It made me remember how me and Mam used to sing and dance around the place when I was much smaller, and I began to realise what a long time it had been since I'd heard her singing or seen her dancing. How far away it felt since we'd had any music in our lives.

'I'm interested in learning to play the piano,' I told Vlad.

70

'OK.'

'If I could get a keyboard, it would be enough. I could make a start. Ninety-nine euros.'

'OK, good. You have target, and target is specific,' he said. 'So if you need to make money, first you need to find rich people. Two things rich people hate: long grass and dirty windows,' he explained. 'Also, grass does not stay short and windows do not stay clean – not for long, so not just once off. Much repeat business.'

Vlad reckoned I could charge up to fifty euros for cleaning the windows of any decently-sized house. It wouldn't take too long to raise the money I needed.

'You have bank account?' he asked.

'No.'

'OK, you must get one. Rich people they never have cash. Only cards and bank transfers, and stuff like that.'

'But I don't know any rich people,' I said, forgetting completely about Violet.

'Of course you don't, so you must broaden your horizons. You will only get loose change from people around here. Only rich person is old woman next door and she never answers.'

I didn't say anything about how well I knew Violet by then. I sort of liked it that she was my secret.

'You must have a bigger vision, sail in a wider ocean! You must go to the other side of town, down by the sea. Start with Mollchester Road. Those people are stupid with their money. You could name a price. You are light and fit and you will be good.'

'But won't they already have window cleaners?'

'Maybe yes, maybe no. And in any case, even if yes, they always complain. Always looking for someone better. So this is what you do. Get yourself over to Mollchester. Offer your services. Keep your prices high. Those people won't haggle you down. They like to think they're paying a premium for something special.

'I lend you my telescopic step ladder. The rest is simple – cloths and a wiper. Some vinegar. Some soap. I give you lesson.'

Twenty minutes of training was all I needed from Vlad before he said I was ready. 'That's it! Simple. So what are you waiting for? Go do it!'

When I arrived on Mollchester Road my face was covered in sweat. Vlad's ladder was light enough but I had to carry a bucket and cloths and a window-cleaning plastic blade and together it was a lot of awkward things, and they nearly didn't let me on the train for safety reasons, and it was a bit of a walk from Mollchester Station.

There was no answer from the first door I knocked on. I trudged up the steps of the second house and before I had rung the bell a cool gust of air blew across my face as the door opened, and a man in overalls told me they didn't have any need of additional help here, thank you very much. And before I had a chance to speak at the third door, a frightened-looking woman came out from a side entrance and said, 'Go away. Please go away.'

'What's this? You no begin your business?' Vlad said when I called round to return the ladder.

'I tried, Vlad, but it wasn't worth the trip. Nobody's interested.'

'What you mean?'

'It was a failure. One woman thought I was a burglar, I think. I was afraid she was going to call the police.'

'You went like this?' He pointed at my head, my t-shirt, my tracksuit bottoms and my shoes.

'Like what?'

'In these clothes, with your hair all down round your shoulders and everything rattling around you like a rag and bone man?'

I didn't think I looked too bad, I told him, especially considering how warm the weather was.

'Oh no, no, no, Penny, you should have come to me for more advice. You need to listen.'

'Thanks Vlad, but I think I'll forget it to be honest.'

'Forget it? After the intention has been set, and the goal is so clear?'

He gave me a pen and paper so I could take notes. 'If you want anyone in Mollchester to trust you, this is what you need to do. You must look a certain way. You must appear to be more like them and less like . . . well, less like you. You must pretend somehow you don't really need the money. You must give off the feeling you just have an unusual interest in window-cleaning, that it's more like a hobby, or for charity. Rich people want to feel like they have something in common with you before they can be comfortable to pay you for a job and let you in their homes. You must make sure your clothes don't smell of The Flats. Try fabric conditioner – and airing your clothes outside. Expensive socks. Make sure they match. Rich people almost always want you to take your shoes off when inside their home.'

I borrowed the money from Matt and promised to pay him back. I ordered bargains on eBay. Second-hand designer stuff. Sports casual. Original Converse runners on my feet, and Tommy Hilfiger shorts and a Lacoste t-shirt. I'd no idea whether this was going to make me seem more like the people I was trying to impress, but when I showed up at Vlad's for an advance inspection, he said, 'Yes, this is better.'

I put my hair in a ponytail. It deserved another try.

*

And when I walked up the steps of number four, Mollchester Road, and a woman swished open the door, this time I said, 'Hello, I was wondering if you needed someone to wash your windows? It's a service I am doing around the neighbourhood for a small fee, in aid of charity.'

'Please do come in,' she said, and I did.

There was a fresh warm-bread smell and coffee in a glass pot on a white kitchen counter. And you could see from the way she was talking, the woman didn't really have a clue how nice her house was – the richness of the air was like roasted nuts and berries and perfume and there were four expensive pairs of shoes in a rack in a small side room.

'It's excellent timing, yes indeed, it really is. I'm Connie Minton-Holmes. You may leave your shoes here.' I shuddered, thinking how easily I might have worn cheap socks if it hadn't been for Vlad's advice.

'Can you really do all the windows with just this tiny ladder?' she asked, striding through the house, me practically running to catch up.

'No problem,' I lied. 'I am very experienced.'

She showed me where and how the newspaper should be laid to protect the floors from any window-cleaning liquid. I assured her I wouldn't leave a single trace.

And all through our conversation, and while I nodded at her, the thing that was already lit inside me began to burn brighter. I can still remember the clean smell of her clothes and the freshness of the rooms, all rinsed in mint and vanilla.

'I think you should start with Millie's room,' said the woman. 'She's home for the weekend, but she's been out by the pool all morning and if I know my Millie she'll be there until lunch, Facetiming her friends who she's spent all term with and who she'll be seeing again on Monday. Seriously! What is that about? So off you go. You shall be able to work away undisturbed.'

The walls of the bedroom were dove grey and the curtains were creamy and thick and there were white painted shutters on the windows. The sun shone through in long rectangular strips, making the pale green carpet look like it had been laid with evenly-spaced yellow bricks. There was a wide desk with purple notebooks neatly stacked and a bunch of pens all packed upright in a pink pottery jar.

I pulled open the shutters and laid the paper and began my cleaning – and I was glad of the practice I'd done with Vlad. I washed Millie Minton-Holmes's windows and dried them and buffed them and polished them, and somewhere in the house I could hear music too.

Just as I was finishing and wondering which window I should do next – and worrying that Connie seemed to have disappeared so I couldn't ask her – I glanced up to the grey wall next to Millie's puffy pink bed. There was a photo there in a wooden frame. When I saw it, and realised what it meant, there was a taste in my mouth. A taste of shock and of envy.

Three rows of girls with hockey sticks in their hands and casual, easy smiles on their faces. There it was: the crest in the top corner with the open oyster and the pearl shimmering inside.

I was standing in the bedroom of someone who attended Pearlbourne Academy for Exceptional Girls. The place I'd already begun to dream about.

I washed the rest of the windows in a cloud of anger and jealousy.

'There are better houses and there are better lives,' I whispered to myself, seething now. 'And there is a school called Pearlbourne Academy with beautiful grounds and horses and music rooms where people go to develop exceptional talents.'

When I was finished, my equipment carefully stacked at the side of the house, I strolled down to the swimming pool, my teeth clamped together, my fists clenched.

Millie Minton-Holmes was beautiful of course, with honey-coloured skin and dark sunglasses on her face and white earbuds nestling neatly in her perfect ears. She waggled her candy-apple toenails in time to the music. I stood close by and watched. She was stretched out and sleepy, slowly flipping the expensive pages of a huge magazine. I wanted to say hello, to come face-to-face with a real live Pearlbourne student, but she did not see me and in the end, my courage failed me and I turned around without her even noticing, and walked back to the house. I wrote out my IBAN on a scrap of paper and left it on the white counter beside a vase of lilies. There was a stack of business cards in a silver stand. It had Minton-Holmes written across the top with the address and their email and their phone number. I plucked one of the cards out and slid it into my back pocket. Then I slipped out and gathered up all my stuff, trying very hard not to be too clanky and awkward, and I headed back to the side of town where I belonged.

Connie Minton-Holmes lodged a payment into my new bank account straight away. It was the best feeling in the world to see €50 flash up on my balance inquiry.

Matt and Kitty texted me as often as usual in the days that followed, but my mood had grown strange since I'd got my glimpse of another world. I spent a lot of time alone in my room, thinking about Millie and her big pale house of soft carpets, with a swimming pool at the back, and Pearlbourne and pianos and other things that were out of my reach.

I rang the Minton-Holmes house a couple of weeks later.

'Oh yes, hello, I'm so relieved you got in touch,' Connie's velvety voice cooed down the phone. 'It wasn't until after you'd gone I realised I'd no way of reaching you. You did such a splendid job on the windows.' She asked me when I could come back again.

Vlad was delighted when I told him. 'See? What did I tell you?' he said, as if he had taught me the secrets of the universe.

So I was back again, this time knowing to take my shoes off and where to put them and which room to start in. When I took a break and went out to the pool, Millie was not there. There was a cover on the surface of the water and the sun lounger had been put away.

I told Millie's mother nothing about myself, just as Vlad had advised. I spoke only when absolutely necessary, in one- or two-word answers. It was hard work, but it was worth it. After two visits, I had enough. I used to like going down to the village just to look at my balance. *Would you like to make a withdrawal?* No. I want to keep it there and use it for my keyboard. It felt so good to have earned money by myself and to be able to buy something I wanted.

I tried to forget about Millie.

I bought my new keyboard for ninety-nine euros. I took it back to The Flats in its box, carrying it under my arm, stopping once or twice to switch sides.

'I'm proud of you, Penny, love, I really am. You wanted it and you went after it and you got it. Well done,' Mam said absently.

'We haven't seen you in ages,' moaned Matt and Kitty, sitting on the stairs one day as I was rushing past. 'What have you been up to?'

I told them about my window-cleaning gigs over on Mollchester and about how good the money was. But that wasn't the only reason I'd been avoiding them. More and more I wanted to be on my own. I didn't want to think about wrestling in the hallway, or Frisbee in the back yard or sausage sandwiches in Matt's flat. I wanted to think about other things: cool, expensive houses, beautiful music. Plus from now on, I was going to need all my spare time to teach myself the keyboard since I'd pretty much decided I was going to be a pianist.

The keyboard came with a stand, same as an ironing board does. I set it up in my room. I searched YouTube to see if I could track down the music I'd heard floating out of Violet Fitzsimons's house – no luck. I found Beethoven's Moonlight Sonata, which was similar, and decided to start there. It was very hard and at first I thought it was going to be impossible. But I grew obsessed. I watched videos about how to read music and how to understand music and how to teach yourself piano. I was going to make myself learn and I'm still not completely sure why, but that was the firmest decision I think I'd ever made in the whole of my life.

Soon, Mam thought I'd grown pale and wondered if there was anything wrong. Which was ironic coming from her because she was the one who was constantly coughing, but any time I mentioned this, she always turned the conversation back on to me.

'Have you been eating properly?' she'd ask, holding me by the shoulders and peering into my eyes. 'Do you have a temperature? Are you sick?'

It wasn't sickness. It was more like an ache, or maybe a hunger. A hunger for the sound of piano, a longing for the glittering air of Violet Fitzsimons's house, a yearning for a different life.

CHAPTER 7

There was an online teacher whose name was Pietro Dastable. He uploaded free clips specially designed for people who were trying to teach themselves. He specialised in the Moonlight Sonata. 'The piano is an impossible thing to master properly,' he said into the camera, 'and so every time someone actually does master it, it's a kind of miracle.' His old face grinned. It felt noble and exciting to be trying to achieve an impossible miracle.

'Start with one piece,' he encouraged and even though he had nearly half a million views, I liked to imagine I was his student and he was my teacher and he was speaking only to me.

In the beginning I was clunky and clumsy and stilted. I went to Blackrock Library and got out books on how to read music. I learned that as well as the different notes, there's something called tempo, and words like *accelerando*, and *andante* and *agitato* and *amoroso* and *con anima* and *doloroso* and *legato* and *volante*. And they are lovely words, and they all mean something different and you can play the same piece in different ways. You have to learn the mood as well as the sound.

I practised hard and I didn't think it would ever happen, but one day, I could feel my playing getting smoother and it was a great feeling. It took a huge amount of repetition to be able to do the first half of the first movement. That's as far as I got. I couldn't do the second or the third, which seemed as if they would always be impossible.

Practising at night was best, when Mam was working. And I did more window cleaning so I could get some good value earphones in SuperValu so none of the neighbours would complain – I was especially worried about Kitty's mam. But one day, not long after I bought them, I lost them. I think they might have fallen out of my pocket on the way home. Or maybe someone stole them. Anyway, the next weekend when Mam was trying to sleep, she said I was making a desperate noise altogether and forced me to take the keyboard and its stand out into the back yard.

'Right down to the end there, where no one can hear, where you won't do anyone's head in.'

This is what I was doing, trying my best to play the Moonlight Sonata in the warmth of the evening sunshine, when I heard Violet's voice calling me from the other side of the wall.

'Hello? Excuse me? Hello?'

There was the squeak of a ladder and her head popped up over the wall, wearing what seemed like a large beekeeper's hat – pea green with netting all around it.

'Wow, Violet, hello,' I said, looking up at her, shading my eyes from the light.

'Oh golly. It is you, Penny Nolan! I thought as much. What are you playing?'

'The Moonlight Sonata.'

'Right, I see, and what are you playing *on*?'

'It's a Yamaha PSR,' I told her.

'In that case, would you mind calling in to me again, as soon as you can please?'

'To your house?'

'Yes, exactly what I said. Right now, if it's possible.'

'Will I bring the keyboard?'

'Do not,' she replied.

When I got to her front door it was open. I walked in on to the shiny floor and through the lavender air.

'Hello? Violet, are you there?'

She came rushing into the hallway, still in her green netty hat.

'Oh gosh, come in, come in, dear Penny!' she said, lifting off the hat. 'I wondered if you'd ever call again, but hearing you play just now made me realise I must take the bull by the horns and invite you,' she said.

Bluebell appeared then, twirling slowly around one of my legs, and then the other.

'Oh, look!' said Violet. 'The queen greets her saviour!'

I gave Bluebell a little scratch on the top of her head, not quite sure what to say next.

'I suppose you know why I've asked you to pop round?' Violet said.

'Is it about the music?' I asked.

'Yes, yes, indeed it is. Now, would you like to follow me?'

She seemed taller, and quicker on her feet than she had been the last time. I knew where she was taking me: to the room I had only glimpsed before now. The room where the black piano glistened, waiting.

It was magnificent. Everything yellow and gold, and a massive soft sofa, and the piano in its own space with a stand. I noticed the green candle flame dancing in the big bay window.

She asked me to sit at the piano. I breathed in and touched the shining wood, then brushed my fingers on the silky keys. They did not feel anything like the ones on my plastic keyboard.

'Do you want to give it a go on this?'

There was nothing in the entire world I wanted more. I closed my eyes for a second, the way I'd seen the online pianists doing. And I began, and I didn't stop until I'd got to the end of the first movement. By then I felt like I was made of music myself.

'That's as far as I've got,' I said.

I looked over at Violet who was sitting on the sofa, her hands over her face.

'What do you think?' I asked.

At first I wondered if she was ever going to answer me, or if perhaps she'd fallen asleep sitting up. A silence stretched between us, and the echo of the sound of my playing seemed to be hovering still above us both.

'What do I think?' She took her hands away from her face and looked very intensely into my eyes. 'Oh my goodness, Penny. That was absolutely . . . absolutely . . .'

'Absolutely what?'

'Dreadful. Appalling. Who on earth taught you to butcher such lovely music in this way?'

It was a terrible moment. I felt stupid and naïve and pathetic. All my hope and purpose evaporated into the air. How could I have been so stupid, playing the piano all proud in front of Violet like that – Violet who knew about music and who knew what it took to be a proper musician? Suddenly I didn't want her looking at me. I wanted to run away and never come to Lavender House again. I wished I wasn't crying but I couldn't help it.

'Oh no, no, what is it, dear girl?'

'Nothing,' I mumbled, sniffing and bowing my head. 'I'm just upset.'

'Goodness, you mustn't be upset. I didn't mean to sadden you so. Oh, but I can see that I have. Silly, stupid Violet!

What I was trying to do was challenge you but of course, typical me! I've been clumsy and harsh.'

I cried even more then. I wasn't able to stop. And I didn't notice her gently moving across the room to sit beside me on the wide piano seat until she handed me a fragrant hankie. I breathed in the smell. Lavender, of course.

'I'm afraid it all comes of the kind of training I have had. Tell me. Tell me why you are so distraught.'

'I heard you playing,' I hiccupped. 'Violet, I stood outside in the front and I listened to you months ago, and ever since I've been longing to be able to play myself. I went all the way to Mollchester Road. It was exhausting.' I blew my nose into the hankie. 'I washed people's windows so I could get enough money for the keyboard. I've been trying to learn on my own and I only had YouTube clips and this whole time I've been worried I have no talent and now I have proof.'

'Proof? What proof?'

'Proof that I am awful – all I've done is ruin the lovely music, just as you've said, and I don't even know what I'm doing here wasting your time.'

'You don't have a teacher?'

'No. Only people on the internet.'

'You're self-taught?'

'Yes.'

'Well goodness me, but this puts an entirely different spin on things.'

I didn't know what to say.

'I expect you could do with a cup of tea,' she said and I nodded. 'Good. Take a few deep breaths and gather yourself a little and I shall be back in a moment.'

It was nice to sit in the comfortable silence of that wonderful room. When she came back she carried a heavy tray. I jumped up, feeling bad for not having offered to help, but she hushed me and told me to sit again. She handed me a gold-rimmed cup and saucer. Her pearl bracelet clinked. I took a sip.

'Certainly, if you've got this far all by yourself, however awkwardly, it tells me you have a fire inside you, which is more important than anything else.'

'But my playing is awful.'

'Yes but you haven't had the benefit of the thousands of pieces of guidance you need. I don't want you to be discouraged. Under the circumstances I can see simply: you've expected far too much of yourself. You shouldn't have been trying to play such an advanced piece. There is so much to learn. Finger position. Pacing. Emphasis and feeling and all manner of technicalities. It's the classic mistake of the enthusiast, if you don't mind my saying, who often fails to realise you must wade through the mudflats of tedious repetition before you reach the emerald palace of virtuosity.

'Indeed, for someone who has never had a lesson, I rather believe there is a wonderful ability there. How long have you been trying?'

'Two months, more. I've barely let a day go by.'

'Yes, well, when it comes to learning to play the piano, that is the tiniest fraction of the blink of an eye. Have you done any scales?'

'What are they?'

'Ha you see, there!' She started playing long strings of notes, rippling up and down the keys, her lovely fingers a blur of perfect speed and sound.

'These,' she shouted, 'are scales! *Do re mi fa so la ti do, do ti la so fa mi re do.* Repetition. Practice. Scales. Exercises. These are what it takes! The point is, you simply must forget about glorious melody until you've done your conscientious apprenticeship!

'And learning wonderful music takes time. You're not ready to play anything until you have listened to it many times with a special ear. But once you commit for the long haul, then who knows what you could achieve.'

There were secrets inside this wisdom. I became hungry to learn them all.

'And you must forgive me my criticism, but it is important for me to explain: criticism is a form of respect and encouragement, for why would I bother if there was nothing there to develop? It's a teacher's way of telling you: you are capable of so much more, you must raise your ambitions, you must take yourself seriously enough to start at the beginning and give it the time it needs. I am a music teacher. There are many who once would have said I was among the best but, oh the world forgets so easily and all my advocates are dead now. Ah well, yes.'

Violet seemed to drift away for a moment, and looked off through the window at some distant thing I couldn't see.

'Under normal circumstances I'd be expensive, but I have always made it my business to create space for free tuition to students of promise. And so, dear Penny, this is what I would like to do.' She reached inside a large pocket of her silk jacket, taking out a small card. From another pocket she pulled a silver pen.

Piano lesson appointment, read the card in gold-edged print.

4pm Thursdays, she wrote.

'Lessons? For me? Violet, I couldn't . . .'

'Don't be silly, my dear. If you're interested, I would love to be able to do some small service to help you to improve. Besides, I feel it's my public duty. Especially if you're planning to continue to practise out in the open air. Your neighbours will be forever grateful.'

We both laughed then. It was a lovely feeling.

'Do say yes, my dear.'

And I did.

Not only was tuition completely free, it was also to include complimentary tea and snacks. There were two conditions.

'It may seem draconian,' Violet explained, 'but if you

are ever late then I shall be forced to cancel the arrangement forthwith. Punctuality is a sign of commitment. Lateness is a sign of waning commitment and in that event our arrangement shall have to be terminated.

'And one more word, it's important none of the parents of the area ever find out I'm giving free tuition or they'll be traipsing up here in a long queue wanting little Timmy or little Mary to get lessons, and I simply do not have the time. I have chosen you. If you do the exercises I give you, and importantly if you stick to my conditions, then you will make progress. But there are no short cuts. You have to be prepared to work very hard, for a long long time.'

CHAPTER 8

Kitty and Matt were the only ones who knew where I'd been. They were sitting in the darkness on the bottom step when I got back.

'She still hasn't killed you! She didn't trap you or cook you? How did you get away this time?'

'Don't be so thick,' I said.

'What's she like?' asked Kitty.

'She's completely lovely. She gets nicer all the time.' I told them about the tea and the strawberry dumplings with dollops of freshly whipped cream she'd fed me, and the piano lessons.

'My mother's going to die when she hears,' said Kitty.

'No she's not, because you're not going to tell her,' I replied, all twitchy on account of already having broken one of the promises I'd just made to Violet. 'It's a secret. No one's supposed to know about me visiting her. I shouldn't be talking about it to anyone, not even you.'

Matt came up close and looked into my face. 'I think you look a bit pale. Maybe she's poisoning you slowly.'

It was the opposite of poison. Violet had strengthened me with sweet tea, and she'd nourished me with food, and she'd dazzled me with music, making me feel as if my whole body was floating. I marvelled about all those years when her doors and windows had shut out the rest of the world, and when the wall between our homes was high and forbidding. To think if it wasn't for Bluebell and the rat poison, I might never have met her at all.

'Mr Galloway, I need permission to leave class early on Thursdays.'

'What for?' said Galloway in his monotonous couldn't-give-a-damn-about-anyone's-life-especially-not-yours voice.

He was in the middle of drawing angry red lines across our term essays.

'It's quite an important thing.'

'Is that so?'

'Yes.'

'You're going to need to furnish me with a little more detail.'

'It's an opportunity.'

'Again, too vague.'

'Free lessons. In music. There is no charge. But I have to

make it to my teacher by four p.m. every Thursday and there's no way I can do that unless you let me out early.'

He kept on scarring the paper with long, diagonal slashes of red. 'What's the name of this teacher?' he asked.

I told him I was not at liberty to say.

He stopped then, put down the pen and looked up at me from his pockmarked desk.

'Penny, may I ask you a question?'

Of course he could ask me a question. He was my teacher.

'I'm just wondering why exactly you think you're so special that you alone can be exempted from your statutorily required school hours?'

'Mr Galloway, come on, I promise I'd catch up at home, I mean I can do it all myself anyway. I wouldn't miss a thing. I swear.'

'So you're telling me you don't need a teacher to work through the complex maths curriculum? Or detailed literary analyses? Or the complexities of geographical terrain? You can do it yourself?'

'Yes, I can. You know I can.'

'I don't know any such thing,' he replied. 'And you see, this kind of false confidence will get you tangled up in all sorts of trouble. And what's more, Penny, this is not a negotiation situation. You are not permitted to leave early on Thursday or on any other day for that matter.'

I tried to speak but he held his hand between us.

'Ah, ah, ah, now Penny, you have to learn. You're not so

unique, you know. You don't deserve to be treated any differently from anyone else.'

A salty sting of injustice prickled at my eyes. I would not let him see, I decided, turning away. I knew what I was going to do even before I'd left the room.

I was a skateboarder. I could get away from Midgrey fast, whenever I wanted. I was going to disobey Mr Galloway and I didn't even care.

From then on I did leave school early – every single Thursday so I could make it to Violet's lessons. And for all his talk, Mr Galloway never even noticed I was gone.

'Punctuality and presence,' Violet said, smiling, when she saw my face at the door. 'If more people just followed those two simple rules they'd avoid a great deal of sorrow and frustration in life. I do you the honour of opening my doors to your musical passion and talent, and you do me the honour of never being late, and in this way we both honour each other.'

She said she wasn't interested in my school grades, however much I liked to tell her about them. She said they had nothing to do with the excellence she was going to be demanding from me, and I don't know why, but that made me feel good. I kept thinking about how I now finally had a teacher who would not let things go – a teacher who would work hard for me, who'd give me no leeway. 'No quarter given!' as she said herself. She wouldn't tolerate half-heartedness in any of its mediocre guises.

It sharpened me.

You can butcher music very easily. You can make it thuddy and heavy and full of nothing. Or you can make it your rescue and it can find your darkness and light you up. Music is full of little pieces of possible light shining through and above the rhythm. The light depends on the playing.

Violet taught me so much and I loved the way I always wanted to try harder because of her. Bluebell would appear doing her glory walk, winding her way between my ankles and the legs of the piano. Thursdays became my days of magic and I will never forget them.

Meanwhile, letters started coming home from our teachers complaining about the smell. Mam got Dettol and borrowed a scrubbing brush from Breda and she spent nearly all of her day off scouring every bit of the black map off the wall. Then Matt's granddad came and painted it over.

'Problem solved,' said Tony, and Mam was delighted. At least she was until the damp came back, and the new paint began to clot and clump and drip down the wall. When

Michael came to pick up the rent, she showed him into my room and Michael shook his head and said she shouldn't have taken things into her own hands. It was against the tenancy agreement.

'You're not supposed to do repairs without permission. To be honest you've wrecked the wall here.'

Mam was raging. She said she'd get the local council after him because these conditions were disgraceful.

'Calm down, Jesus Christ, relax the cacks,' he said. 'Listen OK, I'll see if I can send someone to sort it out.'

I knew he wasn't going to, and I was right because he never did.

At school, Mrs Doyle was all, 'Oh Penny, might I have a word with you,' and then when I said yes, she was all, 'Penny, I'm wondering if you need to pay a little more attention to issues of . . . of well, the rather unusual odour that seems to cling to your clothes?' She didn't really care about me. She just didn't want kids in the class who smelled weird.

'I get it,' I said to her. 'And look, I'll do what I can.'

From then on, I made an extra-special effort to dry my clothes outside. I set up a line with a pulley and stick. One day after it had been raining and I couldn't put my clothes outside, I texted the school office from my Mum's phone explaining that I was sick. And I skipped next door, and told Violet there was no school. She had no reason to disbelieve me and I spent the day in Lavender House watching old movies with Bluebell on my knee, and practising the piano, and eating strawberry dumplings with whipped cream.

It had taken a few years for me, Matt and Kitty to realise we were the poor kids. And being the poor kids in Midgrey was saying a lot. Mrs Doyle put the three of us together for the project groups. By then it would have been difficult for us to work with anyone else. Each group was given a Greek island.

'Children, there are six thousand of them. And so we have plenty to choose from!' Grace's group got Hydra, and Tom Finnegan's group got Santorini and others got well-known ones like Corfu and Paxos. We got a place called Spetses.

'Spetses?' said Matt and Kitty.

Typical us. Getting somewhere that nobody's ever heard of. In the end, as predicted, I did all the research and all the work. We were supposed to find and describe a typical house on our island. I chose a real nineteenth-century traditional seafront mansion called 'Spiti Tou Kapetaniou', which means 'The Captain's House', and drew a floor plan and sketched pictures of the rooms copied from the internet.

I got the poster cardboard and wrote up all the sections and included all the references. Matt and Kitty said I was a superstar and signed their names on the bottom and I was so used to the two of them by then I didn't even have the energy to get annoyed.

Matt was thrilled with the end result of my work and it was hard to be cross with him. He got us to pretend we actually owned the house, and made us imagine what it would be like to sit in the front room watching the sun come up over a diamond-scattered sea.

'Collective action' is what Breda said we all had to take when it came to the condition of The Flats, and she called a meeting of the residents and stood on the first step of the stairs and everyone looked up at her.

'It's gone deplorable at this stage,' she announced, and everyone nodded their heads.

Every time I arrived at Violet's, Bluebell's green eyes followed me and when I sat at the piano she wouldn't stop brushing against my legs and purring until Violet said, 'Shoo, Bluebell.' Bluebell never responded immediately. She would march away in her own good time, usually after I'd completed a first movement – like she knew I was up and running and it was safe to leave me and Violet to our own devices.

*

I asked Matt's grandparents if they'd ever heard of a place called Pearlbourne.

'Yes,' said Tony. 'Posh school. Girls only. Richies, celebs, those kinds of people.'

'The likes of us wouldn't know much about the likes of that place, nor anyone connected to it,' Breda explained. 'They keep things private. They're different from us.'

'They're no different from anyone except for the tank-loads of cash,' said Tony, rubbing his thumb and fingers together. 'It's all about money – the fees alone would pay most people's rent for the year.'

'Ahoy Madaleina, poss me the hockey boll,' shouted Matt.

'This lobster is jolly good,' Kitty chimed in.

'Filly! Feefee! You are such hoots!!' said Matt.

And the two of them could not stop laughing, and Breda tried not to but she laughed too and said, 'Some skits the lot of you,' turning the sausages, which bubbled and spat on the pan.

CHAPTER 9

In a last-ditch effort to connect with Grace at school again, I asked her for a loan of her pencil sharpener and she said no, and later that day there was a note in my locker. *No offence but please do not come near me any more at school or anywhere else*, was all it said.

I tore the note up and threw the little white scraps away, bits at a time in different bins on the way home. I wasn't going to mention this, not to anyone. Grace is obviously a horrible person, I told myself. And until my Thursday lesson with Violet, I thought I'd put the whole thing out of my mind.

'How are you, my dear?' she asked, pointing to the piano stool and handing me a chocolate biscuit.

'No thanks, Violet,' I said, about the biscuit.

'Is everything all right, dear girl?'

Violet stared at me with her lovely grey eyes and I thought about all the mean things people had said about her over

101

the years, and how untrue those things were, and I thought about the mean things people kept saying about me and my friends, and I'd been trying to tell myself I didn't care, but right there, in Violet's piano room, I realised I did care. I cared a lot.

I told her about everything. About the damp in The Flats and how it made us smell funny and how everyone teased us about it.

I told her about my teacher and how he hadn't let me leave school to come to her lessons but how I left anyway and he didn't even notice.

'Clearly a rotter, on both counts,' she said.

I told her about Grace Grantham, and the note she had left in my locker and how I had distributed bits of it into the bins along Midgrey Road.

'Exactly the right place for such rubbish,' she said.

She handed me one of her lavender-scented cotton hankies and when it was saturated, she handed me another.

'Penny, I am so indignant about all this sorrow you've been enduring. I had no idea.'

'I'm sorry. I shouldn't have said anything. We're wasting all this time and I'm supposed to be here to learn music, not to complain about my rotten life.'

'I don't think we'll have a normal lesson today, Penny. I rather think you may not be feeling up to it. What if I play for you? Let me see. How about Mozart? No, we've had him the last two weeks. A little Chopin? No, rather too fiendish for today's purposes.'

She looked up at the ceiling.

'Hmmm, let me think. For similar reasons let's not go near Debussy or Tchaikovsky.'

Her grey eyes twinkled.

'Aha!' She said it so loudly it made me flinch a little on the stool. 'I know the very thing. Beethoven's Sonata number eight.'

'Don't think I know it,' I admitted.

A look of exaggerated shock fell across Violet's face.

'You don't think you know Sonata eight? Pathétique?'

'I know, it is pathetic. There's still so much I have to learn. But remember you said it yourself. The knowledge of the autodidact is bound to be patchy.'

'You misunderstand,' chuckled Violet, 'I would never call you pathetic. *Pathétique* has quite a different meaning – it means passionate, it means emotional, and it's what they call this sonata. To me, it is a compulsory thing. Every human being should have all its notes emblazoned on their hearts, every turn, every bridge, every glorious moment. I rather feel it a rare privilege to be the one to play it to someone who will be hearing it for the first time. Not a single additional second of your life must elapse. So come on now, up off the stool and make yourself comfortable here. Pour yourself some tea. And do have a biscuit. Today, I shall do the rest.'

103

She took her place on the piano stool and was silent for an awkwardly long time, and the sun shone through the bay window, landing on her like a spotlight.

If you've heard Beethoven's Sonata number eight then I don't have to describe it, and if you haven't heard it then I can't explain. But it's as if someone wise has begun to tell you a story that has no words, only feelings and great understanding. And when it speeds up it's like a hundred people dancing and layers of different themes and threads and notes make you weighted to the ground. You can't move when this music is playing. It makes statues of us all. The dance happens inside you, in a deeper part of you.

'*Allegro di molto e con brio!*' shouted Violet over the music, and I was jolted out of my stillness for a second, practically knocking the tea tray off its table.

'Movement nearly over,' she shouted again, and finished with a glorious *bam, bam BAM*. And was still.

Then she whispered, 'Second movement,' as if there was something coming and I needed to be especially prepared for it.

'*Adagio cantabile*. Here it comes!'

She bent her head like someone saying a prayer and held her fingers over the keyboard and I will never forget where I was, and how it felt and how the air landed on my skin the first time I heard it. Sonata number eight, movement number two.

Adagio cantabile means slowly, songlike. Designed to imitate the human voice in music. But as far as I was concerned the music imitated nothing but itself. All the sadness, all the beauty, all the longing, all the regret, all the hope, all the love, all the imperfection, all the dreams, all the goodness, all the peace – swirling around in the room. It felt to me like Violet's playing was pulling the music out of the walls of her house, bringing an ancient and glorious thing into the room, a thing that had always been there, waiting, but could only be brought to life by the touch of her elegant fingers on the silky keys.

In everyone's life there is a moment – a first. This was mine, and whenever I face anything dark or difficult I will forever bring myself back to it. The soft chair in Violet Fitzsimons's huge piano room and the smell of the strong tea and the sunshine spilling in on top of us and her elegant grace, and the sonata, like colours I had never seen rising in clouds from the beetle-black piano, a rainbow of perfect sound.

With a brilliant kind of grace, Violet's arms rose and fell as the sound kept coming, and the slow, heart-breaking notes were like big tears falling and there was a heartbeat underneath holding up the lighter notes, helping them dance, and there was beauty and lightness and dark and strangeness and tenderness and it was like some mystery was filling me up from the inside, the same way sunlight fills up a room.

When she'd finished, I sat in some distant place. Violet came over and sat beside me. She started to stroke my hair.

'Oh, dear girl.' She smiled, handing me another fresh hankie. 'I know, I know.'

I opened my mouth to speak but Violet held a finger up.

'There are no words for it,' she said. 'There is no wisdom in trying to analyse or explain or describe. This is the very reason music exists. It tells us things for which there are no words.'

Matt and Kitty said I'd grown all distant and zoned-out. It was true. Violet's music. My practising and trying to get better and better. The Flats, and the terrible smell. Midgrey. Millie Minton-Holmes's house and the life she had. None of these would leave me alone.

Thinking about Millie made me feel sometimes as if she was standing somewhere near looking lazily past me. I thought about the languid way she had stretched out on the sun lounger beside the swimming pool and how the pool had bounced and flashed like it was full of jewels. I could hear the mesmerising rustle of the magazine whose pages she had slowly turned. I remembered cleaning her windows, and how she didn't know I was watching her and seeing her Pearlbourne photo on the wall above her desk.

I remembered the way my feet had sunk into the deep carpet of the many pale rooms in her house.

My window-cleaning job became a lifeline. It gave me extra money I'd never have had otherwise. I spent it on trying to look more like someone from Mollchester and less like someone who lived in The Flats. I ordered more second-hand designer clothes off eBay. It's incredible what you can get: I found a pair of Gucci espadrilles for a tenner. And I bid for Ellesse shorts and got them for eight fifty and a North Face long sleeved t-shirt for three ninety-nine.

I'd hoped Millie might be there again on any of my visits but there was never a sign of her. I would look at the photos in her room which were enough to make envy seep into me again like I was being injected with it – cold and hot at the same time.

I thought about her on a Pearlbourne hockey pitch or badminton court, or rowing in one of those thin boats, staying upright and slicing through the silky water as if she had magic powers.

We were supposed to have Wi-Fi in The Flats. It was one of the reasons Michael Graves put the rent up. But the signal was patchy and unstable and kept cutting off and I had to share Mam's battered old laptop. Matt found a corner in the entrance hall where the signal was usually better. One night I took the laptop down there and sat on the floor with it propped on an upside-down crate. *Pearlbourne Academy.* When I clicked on the website, the word PEARLBOURNE floated up the screen and then the word EXCEPTIONAL.

Violins played, and pictures popped up of smooth, flower-bordered lawns stretching down to a waterfront, and those thin boats with eight oars each moving together in perfect time, glinting and flashing in and out of the water like knives. Every picture made me blink: clusters of girls in green overalls surrounded by a walled garden, each holding a palate of paints, dabbing gently at canvasses on stands in front of them. There was an assembly hall lined with dark wood, with light coming in mystical shards through mullioned windows. And a video of the Pearlbourne students, perfect and neat, filing along in graceful lines. No elbowing crowds. No jostling or shouting or screaming or pulling or grabbing.

Long corridors crowded with portraits. Dorm rooms softened and rounded with cushions and fluffy blankets and tartan throws. Classrooms filled with books and lovely spaces and beautiful colours. Laboratories filled with benches and bottles and microscopes and torches.

In the background of the video the tinkling sound of the students' laughter mingled with the music. And as the camera pulled back, the blue of their skirts and the white of their shirts made the girls look like little bright coloured stamps on the landscape.

I stared there in the dark until my eyes stung and my breath got shallow. And on the screen, a door opened as if by itself into a room with pale blue walls and a raised stage in the centre, and a cello leaning on a stand, and warm wooden violas and silvery glinting banjos and purple-faced ukuleles. Next, there was a room filled with trumpets, clarinets and flutes nestling in velvet-lined cases. And then a small passageway to another door with a sign saying simply, *Piano*, and I could only stare. Five pianos. Three uprights, a small grand to the side and a bigger one in the centre with a woman in beige overalls leaning over it. She plinked a key and then listened to its vibration and then plinked it again.

The camera swept around to show a different woman in a tweed skirt sitting in a soft blue chair, horn-rimmed glasses, grey hair scraped back.

'At Pearlbourne we understand that it's not just technical or intellectual skills that matter,' she began. 'We hone our girls' mental attitudes. We don't settle for average. We push the limits of what's possible.'

The camera moved again. Next was the library: huge and multileveled – thousands of books and wooden ladders for reaching them and, in every corner, a girl lying on a white beanbag holding a book in front of her face. And next, an office with a large desk and another smiling woman standing behind it. 'I am Lucina Lucas, head teacher of Pearlbourne. If you think Pearlbourne might be the place for your daughter, please do get in touch.'

The email details floated up, the phone number, the address.

Then the credits started to roll.

Pearlbourne:

It's not just about practice, it's about personality, it's about persistence, it's about passion, it's about purpose.

'Are you still up?' It was my mam, standing at the top of the stairs. She hurried down to where I was sitting, coughing her head off.

'What are you doing here on that thing at this time of night? All this late study. It can't be good for you.'

'I'm not studying. I'm looking at something.'

I showed her the website. She stared, mystified.

'What are you looking at this for?'

'Just curious, I suppose,' I said. 'Have you heard of it?'

She narrowed her eyes.

'Parlburny?' she misread. 'What's that?'

'Pearlbourne,' I corrected. 'It's a school. A very brilliant, fabulous school.'

'Oh right, well whatever it is, you shouldn't be down here on the internet at this hour of the night. You should be asleep. Switch that thing off. Honestly.'

'Mam,' I said, suddenly wanting to tell her the idea that was blossoming inside me. 'Mam, I'm searching.'

'What for?'

'Something better.'

'What do you mean?'

'I mean I hate Midgrey. I really hate it. I'm wondering if it might be possible for me to go to a different school.'

She sat down beside me.

'If I could go to a school like this, I'd be challenged and I'd learn to become the best version of myself. My dreams might be able to come true.'

My mother rubbed her eyes and sighed. She lifted a little strand of my hair and put it behind my ear.

'What's got this into your head, Pen? Is it the time you've been spending at Mollchester? Because you need to stop it. It's stupid. You can be as great as you like. You don't need to go to a big posh place to have your dreams come true. Which is just as well, because we'd never be able to afford it.' She chuckled a little bit and part of me loved her so much then, the way she often did her best to cheer me up, even when it was impossible.

'Pen, listen. Don't be craving and pining in the night, wishing for things you can't have, wanting to go somewhere you can never go.'

'You don't understand, Mam.'

Mam was tired, her patience only stretched so far, and she was coming to the end of it.

'No, you're right, I don't. All I know is that most people don't go round whining about things like this. What do they do instead? They just get on with it. Look at Kitty and

111

Matt. Are they staying up late dreaming about going to a posh school on a hill?'

'No,' I said, knowing they definitely weren't.

'Exactly. They're happy to get along. Your school is perfectly good, and it has everything you need and there's nothing wrong with it. Now do yourself – do both of us – a favour and put this out of your head before it takes root.'

I clunked the laptop shut.

'OK, good girl. Come on. Why don't we both call it a night.'

I told her I'd be up in a minute. But as soon as the sound of her steps had faded, I opened the laptop again and broadened my search, surfing through a hundred websites and photos of the boarding schools of the world: English schools in Sharjah with shining roofs, for the children of expats. Schools called *conservatoires* for the musically talented in Paris. Schools for all-round high-achievers in California with floodlit sports fields and polished stages. Schools for the mathematically gifted in Russia with compulsory evening chess.

I listened to the clear, confident voices of students talking and I repeated some of the sentences they spoke. 'This educational experience has imbued in us great confidence and poise,' said one girl from Pankhurst College in Sussex.

'I feel the curriculum has really played to my strengths,' said a tall, tanned boy from Clonadeer School for Boys.

'Sharjah International really gives us an advantage over

112

our contemporaries elsewhere,' said a smiling girl with a headband and a hockey stick.

The education here has been my life's most precious gift. They have realised my potential. I have reached levels of excellence I could never have imagined. It was three in the morning before I crept upstairs and into bed, but I could not sleep for hearing those voices – voices of achievement, voices of entitlement, voices of privilege.

CHAPTER 10

I look back now on the time I spent with Violet in Lavender House as if it was a holiday, or a dream. She lit something up in me and I lit something up in her. It's like I'd known her already, all my life, or in another life maybe, lived a thousand years before this one.

One day she asked me to fetch a special organic pouring cream for Bluebell. I spent ages in Blackrock going in and out of shops before I found it and when I came back holding the little pot of cream in front of me like a trophy, Violet cheered.

One day she said she felt a strange kind of despair and she thought it was to do with how the silver in her home had tarnished. 'Dull as lead or pewter, and to think it used to be so glorious.' The next time I did her shopping, I picked up a big bottle of Silvo. She was delighted.

Getting through all the silver had been a huge task. The Silvo came in a grey bottle with a screw top that made a whispering sound when you opened it. We poured pink wobbly liquid discs on to J-Cloths and we spread them carefully over her silver things: goblets and knives and cups and picture frames and candlesticks. It dried into a pale chalky film and then we rubbed it off and shone the silver until it caught the light and gleamed into our faces, blinding us for seconds at a time. Soon Lavender House twinkled from its corners and its ledges and its shelves.

'This really is quite marvellous!' said Violet, clasping her hands. 'The silver shines at Lavender House again! Hurrah!'

It was pretty much impossible to keep her in books even though she already had a library full to overflowing with them. I lost count of the number of times I went to the bookshop for her. I dusted her old books and catalogued her new ones.

Because of her work shifts and sleeping habits, Mam didn't really notice how much time I had begun to spend there. She never asked me where I was or worried about how long I disappeared for. Kitty and Matt stopped making jokes about the dungeon and the mantraps.

I liked how I was still able to keep Violet to myself. It wasn't just Violet the person, it was Lavender House the place, full of brilliant stuff. She wasn't too enthusiastic about telling me more about Pearlbourne – afraid she might make me bleak with longing – but I begged her to give me all the details. I told her it would make me happy to hear about her days there.

'The pies. Oh, the Pearlbourne cherry pies. An ancient recipe. Always served on Sundays. With cream or custard but never both of course which would have been unladylike. I suppose such ideas are old-fashioned now, but manners and civility were essential then. Part of it was the hundreds of years of tradition, how things were done a certain way because of history. The customs were unassailable and always had to be observed.'

I wanted her to explain.

'Well, for example, every term we voted for our class prefect. It was considered a wonderful honour, and the chosen girl would have special privileges, like extra cherry pie or first choice of horse, or time off campus to go shopping in Clarenbridge and whatnot. Along with the prefect privileges came responsibilities and obligations. As soon as you were voted in you immediately had to start planning, because you had to host a party in your own home during the holidays before your term of office began. I was voted in. Five times! Imagine it!'

She spread her long fingers out like a fan.

'Yes, Lavender House has been host to no less than five Pearlbourne Prefect Parties. Made my sister quite cross – who always had to help, but never got the honour or the glory of the position.'

I'd forgotten she had a sister. Rosemary. But I remembered then how The Flats were originally named after her. I asked Violet to tell me more about her but Violet didn't hear.

'Picture us! All those girls of old. Three times it was a Christmas party, and twice a summer one, and every single one a triumph. All of us gathered together here in this very room, playing piano, and singing songs and rushing in and out. Just us and our youth and our promise and the Pearlbourne spirit.'

Violet sprang to her feet. She smoothed the back of her skirt as she sat on the piano stool and began to play a simple tune. When she started to sing, she closed her eyes.

'Hearts of grit and hearts of fire,
Never waa-aaver, never tire,
Fly the Pearlbourne flag wi-ith pride,
Truth and kindness doth a-abide.'

Maybe her voice was thinner and reedier than it might have been when she was young, and it seemed to crack once or twice, but it had strength and certainty too and when she opened her eyes again it looked as if there were flames inside them, burning.

'I haven't sung it in such a long time, but gosh, how familiar those words, how we shouted them out at hockey and at the regattas and during badminton league and at the Easter and Christmas recitals.'

I thought about my own school with the dead-eyed teachers and Grace Grantham, and its grey walls and the daily scramble for the lockers, and the jungle of mockery in the schoolyard, and the emptiness of my heart when I went in every morning and the blankness of my soul when I came out. And I thought about Pearlbourne with its rolling lawns and its tennis courts and its maths garden and its music rooms and pianos, and more and more I imagined what it would be like to be a Pearlbournian. What it would be like to have a heart of grit and fire, how it would feel to wave the Pearlbourne flag with pride.

I kept all my promises to Violet about the music. I learned my scales and I practised and practised because I wanted her to be proud of me. And even though it made me happy and gave me a new kind of purpose, most nights I went to sleep with the voices of Pearlbourne girls in my head, voices that boasted about feelings I would never feel, talked about experiences I would never have, enjoyed chances I would never get.

It took a few visits to the Pearlbourne website before I noticed the 'archives from the past' tab, and not much searching before I found a ton of pictures of Violet. It felt exciting to see the young version of her, so tall and beautiful and sparkly-eyed, standing under a big arch with the school's name engraved on it, or in the front row of a hockey team, or playing the piano on a stage alone and spot-lit with a black velvet ribbon in her wavy long hair.

And then I came across one that looked like an illusion.

Young Violet laughing, her head held back and a hand in the air, the other holding the hand of another girl who was also laughing, looking at her, but she was also Violet. Two faces, exactly the same. The same set of eyes, the same brightness and the same curves and shades and tones.

'Of course,' I sighed, remembering. One of them must be Rosemary. When I looked more carefully, I could see the face on the left had more freckles and slightly messier hair, and her fingers weren't quite as long.

One Saturday I was clattering my way back into The Flats with my cleaning equipment, fresh from another stint at the Minton-Holmes's.

Kitty was crouched over her phone on the bottom step, locked in some feverish online game. Matt was eating a sandwich.

'Hey stranger!' he said, his cheeks misshapen. Kitty sat up and looked at me.

'How's the window business going? Why won't you let us come with you?'

'I can't afford you. My profits are tiny enough already.'

'We've organised a meeting,' Matt said.

'What about?' I asked.

'You. We never see you. We think you're avoiding us. And it's an emergency because we can't afford to be minus a friend. It means we'll only have each other which would be a social disaster for us both,' explained Matt. Kitty nodded glumly beside him.

'Where's the meeting on?' I asked.

'This is it. It's on here. We've been waiting for you so we can start,' Matt said.

'Guys, come on, there's no need for this. It's just I have a lot on my mind these days.'

'Like what?' asked Matt.

It was time to let them in on the things that had been swirling inside my head. They were my friends. It was only fair.

'If you wait here, I'll show you,' I said and ran upstairs for the laptop. I rushed back down and pulled up the Pearlbourne site.

'This is what's been distracting me. It's a school.'

The Pearlbourne words came floating up: *Paulatim Progressus.*

Kitty and Matt peered in from either side of me.

'What's that?' said Matt, still munching.

'It's a motto. A school motto. It means gradual progression.'

They stared some more.

Pearlbourne: fostering exceptional girls since 1789.

'Does our school have a slogan?' asked Kitty.

'Midgrey Secondary: Boring the arses off children since 1983?' suggested Matt.

'Exactly, you see, that's my point,' I said. 'There are better schools than Midgrey. The people who go to

Pearlbourne carry a literal badge of honour for the rest of their lives. They're invited back for reunions year after year and all they can remember is a million brilliant, happy moments. Everyone gets her name engraved on a thing called the old girls' wall. Look.'

I clicked on a video clip I'd watched – of a glamorous woman in a cashmere coat pointing a leather-gloved finger at the gold-engraved name on the wall, her eyes glistening.

'Imagine liking school as much as that?' marvelled Kitty.

'I know,' I said.

'My name's engraved on a wall in Midgrey,' announced Matt quite proudly.

'Where?' said Kitty.

'On the inside door of the toilets just beside the canteen.'

'OK, shut up. Look at this,' I said.

It was the head teacher, Lucina Lucas. '*Paulatim Progressus* is special to us, and has guided our philosophy from the beginning of the history of Pearlbourne. It means many things. It means there are no short cuts in life. It means regular practice conquers random bursts of energy every time. Much like the beating of the human heart, slow and steady is better than fast and haphazard. No quick fixes. No magic bullets. No easy secrets to success. Dedication and hard work every day. This is what we believe at Pearlbourne. This is what we imbue our girls with, and it stands to them – not just while they are here, but into their futures and for the rest of their lives.'

'What's all this for, Pen? Are you doing a project or what?' Kitty asked then.

'Kind of.'

'Oh no, did Mr Brownlow set it? How soon is the deadline? How come nobody told me? What have I missed? I can't afford another F! Mam'll go furious.'

'It's not a school project. It's my own personal mission, guys. I'm trying to find out as much as I can about this place, because . . .' I paused to make sure the two of them were listening. 'I have this idea I might be able to go there.'

'But you go to a school already. With us. You're a Midgrey student.'

'Exactly the point,' I said. 'I don't want to go to Midgrey any more. I want to try to go there.'

'Don't be mental,' Matt said. 'That place is only for, you know, like if your dad or mam is an ambassador or a millionaire or a politician or something.'

'I know, but there's a scholarship programme. Look.'

Every year we offer a place to a child of exceptional ability who might not otherwise have the opportunity to attend Pearlbourne. For the successful candidate, it is the chance of a lifetime. Here they will be mentored by the best teachers in the world in a climate of pure focus and high excellence so as to realise potential that, without this extraordinary chance, might for ever remain buried inside them.

When Kitty and Matt are lost for words they always start wrestling each other to the ground and then laughing hysterically, which is what they did just then, until Vlad walked through the door covered in plaster and said, 'Hey, too much rough. Bring it outside.'

So they went out to the wild yard and I followed them. They managed to take their wrestling match to new levels of violence until they got tired and then the three of us sat on the ground.

'I've been bored and sad and stressed in school since the day I arrived. I love the idea of going to a place where I could really put myself to the test, you know?'

'S'pose,' Matt said, 'but like, what exactly for? Packing up and going away from your mam and from us, and sleeping in a big room with a load of strangers and never being able to tell anyone what you fancy for your dinner? Doesn't really sound like a bowl of cherries to be honest.'

'It's different for me,' I tried to explain. 'I have a really specific goal now, and without this place I don't think I'll ever reach it. I want to go to university and study music theory and be able to hear the exact sound of notes in my head just by reading from a written score and play in front of a live audience.'

Kitty and Matt both stared at me, blinking and blank-faced.

I thought about my mam and her tired face and her overalls. And I thought about Matt's grandparents cooking mixed grills and the way the smoke always tumbled into the air from their standalone oven. I thought about the huge damp shapes on the walls and the smell of our clothes and how black mould makes people sick.

'Don't you ever want to get out of here? I mean, is this what you want for yourselves for now and for always?' I pointed at the cracked concrete ground and the overgrown tufty grass and the broken-framed windows.

Matt said, 'It's not as bad as you're making it sound. You have to live somewhere. It's a roof over our heads, isn't it?'

'There are a lot of people who'd love to live here,' said Kitty. 'Some people would think this was a palace. A lot of people wouldn't mind going to school at Midgrey too.'

'OK, well, I'm glad you're both happy. But I reckon we deserve better than this.'

'And going to a different school will solve all those problems?' asked Matt.

'Yes! Exactly.'

'My granddad says everyone stands in the middle of their own acre of diamonds already if they'd only stop and look around.'

'Strange acre. Strange diamonds,' I replied.

'Not the point, Pens. You have to be happy inside yourself first.'

'No offence, Matt, but you two don't have the dreams I have. My sort of dreams don't come true. Not in a place like this, I mean. Not in a school like Midgrey.'

'How do you know? They might. Maybe you just have to keep giving it a go.' And Matt gave me one of his heart-breaking smiles, and I had to force myself to ignore the way it made me feel.

'I've been giving it a go my whole life. But there are weights on my shoulders here, and they're pressing me down. I need a place that pushes me forward. Which is why I wanted you both to know: I'm going to do it. I'm going to try for the scholarship. What do I have to lose?'

'You have us to lose,' said Kitty, prodding herself in the chest. 'Your friends. The people you hang out with. That's all.'

'Don't be stupid,' I laughed. 'Going to a new school wouldn't mean I'd have to sacrifice my friends.'

'Are you sure about that?' asked Kitty, frowning.

'I'm positive. Look, I probably won't get in anyway.'

'Do you promise you wouldn't leave us behind?' said Matt.

'How can you even think that?'

'You might get all posh and up yourself.'

'You know I'd never.'

'Good,' said Matt, smiling. 'So now we've cleared it up, is there anything you think me or Kitty could do to help?'

We both stared at Kitty who'd suddenly lost interest in the conversation and was on the other side of the yard throwing stones at a can.

'Hey, Kitty!' shouted Matt. 'Get over here and listen. We've to stop slagging Pen about her notions. She's dead serious about trying for Hogwarts.'

I spent a whole month pulling together everything I needed for the application. I mentioned it to Mr Galloway and he said, 'Good luck with that,' in such a disparaging way that I promised myself never to mention it to him again. I had to write a supporting statement and there was a parents' section, which obviously I filled in myself. I created a new email address, pretending to be my mother. I called it NolanParents@gmail.com. There was a drawer in our kitchen with a file labelled 'Penny' where I found my birth certificate and all my school reports. Penelope was my real name. I didn't really like it. I didn't like Penny much either, so decided to use a different version. A version that might sit better with the people of Pearlbourne. I chose Lola. Lola Nolan. And then at the last minute, almost without thinking, I added Fitzsimons to the end. I liked the look of this new name. Lola Nolan-Fitzsimons. That sounded like a Pearlbourne girl all right.

I held my finger over the submit button and Matt and Kitty chanted, 'Go, go, go!' and I pressed send, and we all jumped around the place as if I'd already succeeded and as if the success belonged to the three of us.

*

I told Violet about the photo I'd found on the Pearlbourne website.

'At first I thought it was a mirror or something. You and your sister were pretty much identical!'

'People often used to say it about us,' said Violet dreamily.

'Would you like me to print the picture off, or get it up on your computer and show you?'

'Oh no,' she said. 'I can't bear the internet. It's all such chaos, like a library with the lights out and all the books scattered on the floor.'

'But it's so lovely. Wouldn't you like to get a copy or something?'

'No, my dear, I don't think I could bear it.' Her voice had become so hushed I could hardly hear it. 'We could never get her indoors,' she whispered then, looking out of the window at the garden. 'Wellies and raincoats and horse-riding and digging and planting, those were her kinds of things.'

I wanted to ask her what had happened to Rosemary or where she was now but just as I was about to ask, Violet said: 'She never spent a single night in the house named for her. She and I were supposed to be always next to each other, but alas it was not to be.'

And then Violet lifted the lid of the piano and told me there was no time for any more discussion.

CHAPTER 11

There'd been a terrible scene the last time Kitty's report had arrived. Her mam had thrown a chair at Kitty, who ducked so the chair hit the wall. The mark was still there, behind Kitty's telly. Big hole in the wallpaper, torn and peeling. Kitty's mam had grown less and less predictable, prone to week-long bouts of crying about her future and about Kitty's.

'I've learned my lesson,' Kitty said. 'Better not to upset her.'

Even though she went mental if she actually saw her school grades, somehow Kitty's mam never seemed to notice if they happened not to arrive. After summer tests, which Kitty knew she'd failed, we agreed to take it in turns to be on post-watch for the results. They didn't arrive on Monday when Matt was on duty. It was Kitty's turn on Tuesday, then me, then Matt again. The interception system was straightforward. Keep an eye out for Jimmy the postman;

search through everyone's mail; fish out the school letter addressed to Kitty's mother and destroy it on sight – preferably by setting it on fire out in one of the hidden corners of the back yard.

'You know there's a much better way around this?' I said to Kitty on the Tuesday, as I passed her on the stairs.

'What's that then?' she asked.

'You could actually make an effort to improve your grades, then we wouldn't have to hide the truth from your mam. You know I could help you – all you have to do is ask.'

'You're all right, Pen,' said Kitty. 'I'm grand.'

'You're clearly not grand. I could easily just give you a few pointers. Help you catch up. Show you the basics.'

'Penny, like I say, thanks, but no thanks. It's bad enough to have to do work in class without wrecking every moment of my spare time with it.'

'Oh yes, I forgot,' I said. 'Your spare time and all the superb choices currently available to you.'

'Now you're just being mean,' Kitty said, and maybe I was, but I wanted her to admit that studying wasn't the worst thing she could do, considering that her main occupations included sitting on the broken old steps in the hallway playing with coins and a stick, or curling up inside the dark cave of her flat keeping out of her mother's way locked in an endless game of Fifa, her eyes glazed, her face flickering, in a state of semi-conscious hypnosis. If it wasn't for Matt and me, Kitty would probably never get outside at all.

Lots of people came and went through the main entrance of The Flats. It was important not to make them suspicious. We decided it would look less dodgy if we masqueraded as helpful neighbours dividing up the big lump of mail and delivering it to its owners.

'Saves you rummaging through the pile, looking for your own,' we said, knocking door-to-door, and handing over the bundles, pretending our only motive was an act of charity. I remember how Jimmy was off duty that Wednesday and how by a strange accident the replacement postman posted Violet Fitzsimons's mail into The Flats. I remember looking at the six firm envelopes with her name and address in curled handwritten ink and stamps and postmarks from Paris and The Ivory Coast and Madagascar and New York and Monaco and Los Angeles. I remember running my fingers over the textured paper. Even Violet's mail was interesting and glamorous.

Breda and Tony's post looked more like bills and junk but when I delivered it to them, still they seemed delighted. 'How kind! Isn't she kind, Tony?' said Breda, and Tony said that was just the thing you'd expect from a good-hearted girl like me.

Strictly speaking, Matt's grades weren't much better

than Kitty's but his grandparents didn't worry about things like that, especially now he'd already decided he was going to be a photographer. Photographers didn't need formal qualifications.

'Just an easy way with people, a good eye and an instinct for what's about to happen next,' Tony said.

'Check, on all three fronts!' boasted Matt, and Kitty and I couldn't disagree.

Unlike Kitty's mother, Breda and Tony loved getting Matt's school reports – even though Matt had to read the grades out to them himself, since their eyesight was bad. They glossed over every F as if it wasn't there at all, and responded to every non-F with oohs and ahhs and the call for a celebration. And then they'd cook up a party-sized mixed grill and come out on to the landing to shout a general invitation.

It might have seemed to my friends that the school reports were the focus of that week, and yes, we remained on special guard for Kitty's. But the truth is that by then there was really only one letter I was interested in.

Kitty was on duty the day the Pearlbourne envelope arrived. Shimmering with its oyster crest, yawning shell and the shining pearl inside, bathed in a pinky glow. 'Stand back,' said Matt. 'Let Penny open it.'

I pulled the letter close so the others couldn't see.

Dear Lola Nolan-Fitzsimons,

The panel has considered in detail your application for a
Pearlbourne scholarship. We regret to inform you that you
have not been successful. We cannot enter into any
further correspondence about this matter. We thank you
for your interest in Pearlbourne Academy, and we wish
you every success in your future endeavours.

Yours sincerely,
Lucina Lucas

What was I thinking? Fooling myself that I was getting
closer to it all: the glitter and the sparkle, the music behind
closed doors, the windows shining in the sunshine, the
polished floors, the velvet cushions, the flying flag, the
oyster with its pearly prize. Now the Pearlbourne oyster
had snapped shut and would never be open to me. I wasn't
good enough. I was going to have to forget the whole thing.

'It's a no,' I told my friends.

'Oh,' they said and were silent.

'That place is a pile of crap anyway,' said Kitty after a
while.

'You're too good for them,' said Matt, even though we
all knew it wasn't true.

The reports arrived in the same bundle and mine might
as well have got ripped up and set on fire with Kitty's –
because my grades didn't matter any more. They didn't

carry any special information, or tell me anything I didn't already know – not now that the Pearlbourne dream was dead.

Still, I brought my report upstairs to the flat and left it on the counter, and when my mam got up, she peered down at the paper, as usual seeming a bit unsettled by the consistency of my perfect academic record. I didn't even wait for her to say anything. I just got up and walked into my room and sat down at my desk.

She followed me.

'Pen,' she said, standing in my doorway. 'You know, I think you need to get out more and stop your studying, give your classmates a chance to catch up,' she laughed, only half joking. 'You need fresh air. Go out and play with your friends, why don't you?' She pointed at the window from where I could see Kitty and Matt half-heartedly kicking a football around the back yard. 'You don't need to be blinding yourself with so much work and study. You're doing great.'

I looked up at her from my creaky chair.

'Mam. I'm not doing great at all.'

'Sure, look at it would you?' she said, pointing at my report. 'You can't improve on those.'

I sighed and closed my eyes for a second, then opened them again.

'They're not an achievement. They're a ceiling and I can never get past them.'

She stared at me, squinting like there was thick fog between us.

'I've never heard such rawmation in my life. What ceiling are you talking about? How could you be doing better than this?' She slapped the back of her hand against the report. 'A1s down the line. To be honest it's not even normal.'

'See! That's what I mean, Mam, I don't think I am normal. I'll never be normal or happy, not here. Not in this place or in Midgrey School or in this life. You know there are people who love every minute of school. They go to places where they can fulfil all their potential and they remember nothing but happiness and success in places like that.'

'Sorry, Pen. Sorry your life is so awful. Maybe you've been too busy to notice but I'm doing my best for you. And by the way, anyone who tells you their school days were perfectly happy, well they're either lying to you, or they're lying to themselves.'

I hadn't meant to make her feel bad. I wanted to tell my mam how I hated how hard she had to work, how worried I was about her constant cough. But I'd gone too far already.

I had to shut up now. She didn't even know I'd applied for Pearlbourne. It was wrong of me to blame her now I hadn't got in.

'I'll leave you to it then,' she said, her voice quiet. She shut the door gently and I turned my chair around, leaned my chin on my hands and stared out into the dark.

*

134

Just as I'd begun to think I couldn't feel much more bleakness in my soul, the following Thursday, someone trashed my locker. I'd sneaked out of Galloway's class and was tiptoeing down the hallway to grab my board. I could see it from a distance even before I reached it. My locker door was bent back and all my books were torn and scattered on the floor nearby, and my skateboard was gone. A cold blush of fear flooded through me then because I couldn't be late for Violet. It was her most important rule.

I was a bullet spinning from a gun. Zipping down Midgrey Street, heading to the traffic lights at Parkin's Cross. I cleared a kid in a single jump – no damage done. The woman holding the kid's hand shouted but I didn't stop. Music was playing in my head, very loud. My school bag jangled on my back.

I bumped into a man in a suit. 'Hey, take it easy,' he said. I didn't have time to apologise.

'You're supposed to wait for the green man!' somebody else roared while I dashed across the road at Clancy's. There was a sudden high-pitched sound – a car screeching to a stop.

I could feel the rush of blood through my body and the air in my lungs and the sweat on my skin.

A crocodile of pre-schoolers snaked two by two towards the town square. I dodged and weaved around them.

'WATCH OUT PLEASE, CHILDREN HERE!' yelled their minder, waving at me with both arms as the children stared.

The late afternoon sunshine sliced through the railings. I couldn't bear to check the time as I opened Violet's gates and jogged up the stone path, patting down my hair, straightening my twisted jumper.

I lifted the huge dolphin door-knocker and finally looked at my watch. A full fifteen minutes late. I'd never broken this rule. Her shadow blurred the coloured glass.

'Oh, thank goodness, I was starting to worry!' she said. Her voice echoed in the entrance hall. I followed her across the tiled floor and our footsteps rang out. We turned left into her living room. I held my breath.

'What's this defeated look about? What has darkened your mood, dear Penny? Come and sit down here.' She handed me a cup of tea and held out a plate of her strawberry dumplings, then sat down by the table.

'Violet, I'm so sorry I'm late. It wasn't my fault. My skateboard got stolen.'

At first, Violet gasped and shared my outrage and asked all about how such a ghastly thing could have happened, and then we sat in silence in that wonderful room. It was a while before she spoke again and even though I was expecting it, what she said made me feel sick and shocked and terribly sad.

'Dear Penny, it pains me to tell you this,' she began. I got myself ready, stiffening my jaw and squeezing my eyes shut, waiting for it.

'I'm afraid this is going to be our last lesson for some time.'

I stood up, putting the teacup back in its saucer, trembling.

'Violet, seriously, please, it wasn't my fault. It won't happen ever again. Please don't cancel our lessons.'

'You misunderstand, my dear. Your lateness has nothing to do with this.'

'So why can't I come any more? Have I failed you some other way?'

'You have not failed at all. On the contrary, you have been a wonderful student – and more, you've been such a companion, such a friend. You have filled my life with light again and I cannot explain how much it has mattered to me. I will miss you greatly. My life had faded to black and white, and then you came to the door with Bluebell in your arms and you started to colour my world in again. You've breathed so much life back, my dear. There'd never have been any question of my stopping our classes.'

'OK, so why then?'

'I'm afraid I am unable to speak of why, so please don't ask. All I can say is I shall be shutting up this old place for the time being and I will be gone in the morning.'

'When will you be back?'

'I wish I could say, but I cannot.'

'Maybe if you told me what it was, I could help. You said yourself I've been a great help already.'

'And so you have, my dear, but no. This is a solo journey, I'm afraid.'

'What about Bluebell? Where will she go?'

I could feel the cold brick of loss inside me already.

'I've already placed her in appropriate alternative accommodation.' It was only then I realised I hadn't seen Bluebell; she wasn't nestling in her little bed of cushions by the unlit fire, she wasn't doing her welcome weave around my legs.

'Where?' I asked.

'A good home,' Violet replied, and the way she said it sounded very permanent and very final and I got this feeling that the things Violet wasn't telling me about were serious and dark, and I started to cry, hating myself but not being able to stop. I didn't even bother to wipe my tears away as they slid down my face.

'Oh now, silly nonsense,' she said, pulling a tissue from its white box and handing it over. I blew my nose.

'This is the end of the world,' I said.

'Slight hyperbole, my dear, if I may say so.' She smiled and I tried to pull myself together.

'Please don't leave,' I said again.

'I am afraid I must, dear girl. Now. Don't let's talk about it any more.'

'Violet, being a student of yours has been the best thing ever. How can you take that away from me?'

'But my leaving doesn't mean you have to give up music. You started without me, and you can carry on without me.'

'No I can't.'

'Yes, you absolutely can. You've been doing so wonderfully well. You've come so marvellously far.'

'It's only because of you. Without you, I'll lose the discipline. Everything's going to be dead and grey again. I won't be able to keep going.'

I started to sob then. Could not speak. Felt as if I was crumpling.

'Oh my dear, come, come. What is it? There must be something else going on to make you sob so.'

'I tried to get into Pearlbourne,' I explained between hiccups, like I was a little kid. 'I never told you, but I filled in the scholarship application, and I've just found out they said no and you can't leave me because this is all I have now. If I can't come here and play piano with you, all I'll have is my tinny plastic Yamaha keyboard and all it will do is fill me with longing for you and for Pearlbourne. Violet, my dream is over. I've been dreaming of the place ever since you told me about it and now I'll never play in the Pearlbourne piano room and never row on the Pearlbourne river or perform on the Pearlbourne stage.'

'But why did you not tell me, my dear girl, when I'm the very person who could have helped all along?'

139

'Well it's too late now anyway. I have to accept I'm not exceptional, and I never will be.'

She made a little whirlpool in her teacup with her silver spoon.

'Sometimes the harder you want something, the further away it gets. Letting go can in fact be a good way of allowing something to come to you. Our greatest longings are like cats, you know? When you approach them, they run away. When you sit quietly, playing your own music, feeling your own rhythm, that's when they wander over and sit in your lap. Just wait. It might come to you. When in doubt the best ever thing is not to do anything. Don't make any decisions to give anything up. Just wait, listen, keep your eyes out for an opportunity.'

I didn't know what she meant at the time and I was too sad to notice the meaning hidden in her words. She lifted her glasses hanging on a chain around her neck and perched them on her face and said, 'There is something I would like to do before I go.'

'What?' I sniffed.

'I would like to pay you please for all the work you have done for me these last months.'

'Oh no, Violet, honestly. I liked everything I did here. I liked bringing you your milk and helping Bluebell. I liked polishing all your silver. None of the jobs felt like work. It was all fun. Besides, you gave me all those lessons. You don't owe me anything.'

'Dear girl.' Violet held up her long index finger and she gazed at me with this glittering look she sometimes had. 'Allow an old woman to bestow a small gift on a girl who has come to mean so very much to her.'

I resisted but she kept insisting, asking for my bank account details, and I was proud to have a bank account, even though there were probably only about twelve euros in it. In the end, I checked my IBAN and BIC on my phone, and she opened up a worn leather notebook at a blank page and made me write out the numbers for her.

'Oh good, excellent,' she said. 'Penny, two more things. May I give you a key to the house, and my mobile number, just in case I need you to check something?'

'Of course,' I said and she scribbled down her number and handed me a key on a black velvet ribbon.

'I hope we shall get to spend time together again, but if we don't then still all will be well. You are a wonderful girl. You are not powerless about your destiny. You can have a brilliant life.'

It was kind of her to say it, even though it was not true. All the glimmers of light she had hinted at, all her stories about Pearlbourne Academy for Exceptional Girls, all the teaching she had done to make my playing so much better, it was going to be gone and I'd have to go back to playing computer games with Kitty and Matt.

I followed her to the door and we hugged for a long time.

'Will I not be able to talk to you, even?'

'Of course! Phone me! Anytime at all, you have my number. But for now, it's farewell, my darling girl.'

CHAPTER 12

In the nothing days that followed, Midgrey was a blur of boring sound and meaningless deed. I barely managed to put one foot after the other.

Matt's grandparents' place was warm and as usual there was a mixed grill in the oven. Cooked, glistening sausages, and soft fresh bread in the cupboard and sugar for tea – and the door was always open.

'Tony, get up off the sofa and give Penny a plate, and ask her if she wants a cup of tea. What will she think of us?' said Breda one day when I called after school.

Tony made a move to struggle up from the sofa.

'Don't move, Tony, I've got it,' I told him.

I squeezed by Breda to the kettle, and ducked my head out of the way when she opened the treat cupboard and pulled out a long pack of Twixes.

'Help yourself, love. Sugar to build your strength up? You look a bit shook. Has something happened?'

'I'm OK. Just a bit disappointed about not getting into the school I applied for, and about my skateboard.'

'What about your skateboard?'

'Stolen. From her locker. At school,' said Matt.

'Oh, for goodness' sake, what kind of a gurrier would steal a child's board from under her nose? It's a disgrace. Tony. Tony, did you hear what I said?'

'What?'

'Penny's skateboard. Some no-good rascals have stolen it! What kind of lowlifes are prowling around at all? Why couldn't they go off and rob a bank if they're such big men, instead of taking things away from children?'

Tony made a clicking noise with his teeth and sat up a bit straighter on the sofa. 'A disgrace, is what it is.' The two of them shook their heads.

Kitty arrived and smiled at the sight of us and the sausages.

'She's had her board stolen,' Tony and Breda said together. Kitty stopped smiling and joined in the outrage and the name-calling and I had a big, sudden urge to blurt out how much I loved them, but it would have been weird and embarrassing so I didn't say anything.

'And I was getting free music lessons but they've finished unexpectedly and I'll never be a musician now.'

'Why not? You don't need lessons, girl. I've heard you playing away out in the garden. Sure you're brilliant.'

'I'm not brilliant. I only have raw talent at the moment.

It needs to be honed. I mean, it would be fine if I just wanted it to be a hobby. But Breda, it was my calling. It was my passion. It was my purpose. And it can't be now.'

'What's all this *can't* out of you, Penny, it's not like you,' said Matt. 'Everyone told Beethoven he couldn't be a musician because he was deaf. But did he listen?'

'Haha, good one, Matt,' wheezed Tony, and gently, Breda held my wrist for a second and said, 'Don't mind them, they're only trying to cheer you up.'

'For your information,' I replied. 'Beethoven became a musician long before he lost his hearing, so technically speaking the joke doesn't actually work. Anyway, I'll get over it. Maybe I'm not meant to be a pianist. Maybe I'll decide to be something else.'

The following Thursday afternoon, every time I looked up from my desk, Mr Galloway was looking down at me.

'Still with us then, Penny?' he said and I thought I saw the flicker of a smile on the corners of his mouth.

'What's your point?' I wanted to ask, but I already knew what Mr Galloway's point was.

'Yes, I'm still here,' I said.

'Not packing your suitcases for boarding school? Not leaving to move in elite circles? The plan has changed, has it?'

'Yes. It's changed.'

'Activating Plan B, are we?'

'Whatever you say, Mr Galloway.'

'What happened, Penny? Did you change your mind?'

'No, I didn't.'

'What was it then?'

'I didn't get in.'

'Penny Nolan fails an entrance exam? What a surprise. And what does this mean?'

'It means I have to stay here.'

'Yes, indeed. You'll have to settle for us again now, though it's clear you think we're beneath you. We'll have to be good enough for you, I'm afraid.'

'Yes,' I said.

'Maybe we can rely on a little more engagement and enthusiasm from now on then, huh? Now you don't have another option.'

'Maybe,' I said.

Mr Galloway had given us homework on ancient Greek history. It was the parable of Icarus. As usual, I was the only one in the class who'd done the reading.

'Who's read the story?' he asked us, scanning hopefully over our heads.

I put up my hand. 'I've done it.'

'Well, would you mind giving the rest of these illiterates the benefit of your wisdom?' he said.

'Deadalus was the father of Icarus,' I began. 'He's the one responsible for making the wings. He made them out of feathers, stuck them together with wax. "Listen Icarus, listen to me," he said. "These wings are going to work fine, but there is one thing you must not do." To which Icarus replied, "What is that, father?" "You must not fly too close to the sun." Deadalus paused and looked at his son, thinking they were in the middle of a teachable moment. "What do you imagine will happen if you fly too close to the sun?" "Will the wax melt, Dad?" asked Icarus. "Yes, son. Exactly right," replied his father, who went on to drive the lesson home by explaining if the wax melted then the feathers would fall away from each other and Icarus would tumble from high in the sky to certain death.'

'Very good, Penny,' said Mr Galloway. 'I'll take it from here. And what do you think Icarus said?'

The class was silent with baffled indifference.

'Icarus said, "Yep, got it, Dad,"' continued Mr Galloway. 'But as soon as he got his wings and learned to fly, well, Icarus – bit of a thrill-seeker was our Icarus – he was ecstatic. He was exhilarated. He flew up and up, higher and higher, and forgot all about his father's warning. Fell to his death, right into the sea near Samos. They named part of the ocean after him – the Icarian Sea. So, what do you think's the moral of the story?'

'Don't fly too close to the sun?' I suggested.

'Very good, Penny, and remind me after class, I'd like a quick word.'

After class, he told me pride comes before a fall and most people are not destined to fly as high as they might want to. He said not everyone can have a glamorous, shiny life and I'd be much better off being content with what I already have.

I gave up piano completely. The things I loved about music were gone from me: hope, a vision for something better, happiness, the feeling that if I just kept running forward, I might be able to lift off the ground and soar high into the air. I stopped reading, I stopped studying. I got so good at Fifa that Kitty didn't want to play against me any more. I stopped being obsessed with private school websites, stopped looking at them late at night.

I tried to focus on the positive, like Violet had advised. I had Kitty and Matt. We kicked the ball or threw the Frisbee around the yard, and lounged in the entrance hallway and played videogames, and our clothes kept on smelling of the black mould, and my mam kept falling asleep in front of the TV, and I ate baked beans straight from the can to save on the washing-up.

I deleted the Minton-Holmes's number from my phone and I stopped going to Mollchester to wash their windows or to see if anyone else was interested in me washing theirs. And just when I thought I'd killed the dream completely, early on the morning of Saturday June the fifteenth when a strange rain was pouring down on to the streets of our town, I realised the dream must only have been sleeping, because this was the day my dream woke up again.

CHAPTER 13

There was literally no food in the flat that Saturday. The best I might have been able to hope for, if I was lucky, would be an old onion rolling around in the bottom of the fridge, or a tin we'd forgotten about somewhere in the back of the cupboard, or maybe the last few stale cornflakes at the end of the box. There was no milk in the fridge and no butter on the counter and no bread in the cupboard. I checked the jar, just in case. Thirteen cents. It was Mam's day off but I knew she'd stay in her room for the whole of it. No work. No money. Nothing to get up for. Three days till payday. Might as well go back to bed myself.

I lay looking at the black shape on the wall. I stared at the mottled ceiling. I checked my phone and texted Matt and Kitty but there was no answer from either of them. I picked up the book I'd been trying to read but I just stared at it too. Then I let my arm drop.

It was the thump of the book as it fell to the floor that made me remember: there must still be around twelve euros left in my own bank account. And Violet said she was going to pay me a few quid for the work I'd done in her house and even though I hadn't wanted her to, I was glad now that she'd insisted. I'd be able to get a few things in – maybe make lunch and convince Mam to get up – and she'd be more or less thrilled with me. I'd shop carefully so I could fill the cupboards enough to keep us going until Tuesday.

I grabbed my bank card and the keys, ran downstairs and headed off to the village. It was raining and I'd no umbrella, and I wasn't going to go upstairs again just for a coat, so I hunched my shoulders and hurried down the street to the cash machine at the corner of Lorenzo's and SuperValu. One or two people trotted by. The wheels of a car whirled wetly past, swishing through the gutter. A fan of water drops sprayed into the air.

I slid the card into the machine, muttering at the rain, shivering a little and praying there actually was money in there. I punched in my pin number and pressed for the balance on screen, and then I scrunched my eyes together.

'Please let there be twenty,' I whispered to the machine – a kind of money prayer that never usually comes true. When I opened my eyes, the digits on the screen glowed and swam blurrily in front of me. I put my hands flat on the wall on either side to hold myself up and I squished my eyes together again and kept them closed for a few seconds more. Then I stared back.

€1,042,013.27

'Sorry, what?' I said to the machine as if it was a person.

ONE MILLION, FORTY-TWO THOUSAND AND THIRTEEN EUROS AND TWENTY-SEVEN CENTS?

ONE MILLION, FORTY-TWO THOUSAND AND THIRTEEN EUROS AND TWENTY-SEVEN CENTS?

Keeping my hands flat on either side, I looked around, up the street and down it and then behind me and back at the screen, which had started to flash.

'Do you wish to complete another transaction?' it asked. I pressed yes. Then I pressed the €500 button and waited, listening to the sounds of the machine's clicks and whirrs. 'Take your card,' it said. 'Your cash will follow.' I held my breath and snatched the card, like I was rescuing it from the teeth of a dangerous beast, and shoved it into my back pocket. High in the sky a seagull squawked. Nearby, the bell of a passing bus dinged. The cash machine made a clattering sound and a warm technological gust blew out, and there was a gentle flutter like the wings of a bird. And I could see the clean edges of many perfect notes.

I pulled them out and looked down. Drops of rain landed in plump circles on the top fifty, rolling around and sliding off. I curled all the money into a tight cylinder

152

and wrapped my fist around it and my heart thrashed like a hooked fish and little silver stars flashed and danced at the edges of my vision.

I'd heard about things like this before. I remember reading once that a girl went to court because she spent a load of money that had accidentally been put into her account. This money in front of me was one of those massive mistakes. The bank would realise it soon and take it back and give it to its rightful owner. I plunged the five hundred into my pocket and wiped my hand on my thigh. 'What have I done?' I thought. 'I'm going to be in serious trouble.'

And then I remembered Violet and the unusual things she had said to me before she went away. How insistent she had been about getting my bank details. How she kept saying I was not powerless. And how a wonderful life lay ahead of me. I'd thought it was all just a way of softening the blow of her leaving, but maybe this was what she meant. I didn't have my phone with me. I would call her later. Maybe she'd put more money in than she had intended. We'd figure it out together. 'OK, it's fine,' I told myself. 'I can't put this five hundred back. I'll treat it as a loan. I'll do more windows to earn it back. Might as well spend it on stuff we need.'

I kept telling myself to stay calm, and pretty much stumbled across the road. Near me, a car skidded and beeped and I jumped, then walked into SuperValu as slowly and normally as I could manage, feeling as if there was a siren on the top of my head blaring, loud, making people look at me. I plunged my hand into my pocket, clutching the money. With the other hand I kept checking my back pocket and feeling for the outline of my bank card.

'Em, sorry, do you have change by any chance?' I asked Debbie Feely, who was filing her nails at the checkout.

I turned my back on her and pulled out the roll of money to peel off a single note and then turned and handed her the fifty and she frowned at me and kept staring into my eyes as she doled out the change very slowly. I put a coin in one of the big trolleys, and then began the shop of my life.

Five tubs of Häagen-Dazs ice cream.

Three tubs of Ben & Jerry's.

Four sliced pans.

Six trays of good sausages.

White pudding.

Ketchup.

Brown sauce.

Salad cream.

Cereal.

Four big cartons of Tropicana orange juice.

Chocolates.

One giant bar of Toblerone. Another one.

Crisps and nachos and avocados and sparkling water and a six-pack of tins of beans and cheese and tomatoes and crackers and rice cakes and a watermelon and a pineapple and toilet paper, the kind we never buy, and new toothbrushes and two big butters, a four-pack of Snickers bars. Posh bread with seeds on top and a big box of teabags and a jar of white sauce.

Debbie Feely was still at the tills when I approached with my trolley.

'Are you all right?' she said, snapping her bubble gum and looking at me and then at the trolley.

'Yeah,' I said. 'Why do you ask?'

'No reason, only you look a bit funny,' she said. 'And you're soaking wet.'

'I shouldn't have come out in the rain without a coat,' I said stupidly, and she acted as if this was enough of an explanation and I was relieved she didn't say anything else.

I had to pay for seven 'bags for life' to pack the groceries and then asked if I could bring the trolley home with me since I wouldn't be able to carry this lot back on my own, and she said fine, just bring it back or you won't get your euro and I said grand and then I wandered, distracted, back across the road holding on to the trolley with one hand while I went to the machine just to check the balance one more time. The money was still there.

155

'Do you want a printout?' asked the machine.

The tongue of paper glided out. I grabbed it and shoved it into my pocket and ran and ran and ran, the trolley wobbling and rattling in front of me, back home through the rain, my whole body swamped in a breathless cloud of disbelief.

I struggled inside with the trolley and hid it in the musty dark space under the stairs, and sprinted up to get my phone. I could hear Mam's snores, so I crept carefully, snatched my phone, and headed back downstairs again. I sat outside on the step where the signal was better. The rain had got heavier and harder. When Violet answered, there was a lurch in my heart and a pain in my stomach, just at the sound of her voice, which seemed very far away. 'Violet, I'm sorry if I'm disturbing you.'

'Not at all, dear girl. I'm in an airport. It's enormously tedious. Lovely to hear you.'

'Listen, Violet, you remember how you were saying you were going to lodge some money into my account?'

'Yes, of course I remember.'

'Well, did you?'

'Yes. I did.'

'I think there's been a mistake.'

CHAPTER 14

'Whatever can you mean?' asked Violet. 'Did it not arrive?'

'No, I mean yes, I mean it did, but the thing is . . . It's a very massive amount of money.'

'Oh good. I'm so glad,' she said, not sounding too surprised.

'No, I mean, you've given me too much money. I think you must have made a mistake.'

'How much does it say?' she asked and I told her.

'Did you really mean to send me that much?' I asked.

'Violet Fitzsimons never does anything she does not mean to do,' she replied.

'Oh Violet, I just can't believe it,' I said and I heard her laughing.

'Why can't you believe it?'

'Well it's just . . . it changes everything. So many things are possible now that were impossible before.'

157

'Quite,' she said. 'What will you do?'

'I'm wondering if Pearlbourne might be possible again.'

'Splendid!' she said. 'This is exactly what I hoped you'd wonder and yes, of course it is. You have the means to go under your own steam now. You don't need scholarship approval.'

'But how will I do it?'

'You're a clever girl, Penny. Now that some practical barriers have been removed, you'll find it very straightforward,' she said, as if me going to Pearlbourne was the most natural, unremarkable thing in the world. 'I'm writing you a letter. There is this tradition known as the "Pearlbourne letter of introduction". It's an Old Pearlbournian's privilege – a trusted way of getting someone to the top of the queue, so to speak. Once I've sent it off, a place will be yours and you have everything you need to activate the rest. Is Penny your full name or is it a shortening of something longer?'

'Penelope,' I whispered, not being in the habit of telling anyone this truth about myself.

'Ah, Penelope! Of course, and how wonderful.' I told her that if I was going to Pearlbourne I was probably going to shorten my name to Lola, and she said, 'Thank you my dear, I shall keep that in mind, though of course you will always be Penny to me!'

I was about to ask her how I was ever going to be able to assemble everything I would need, but I stopped, remembering again. I had a million euros in the bank. I could do anything I liked.

A whole new mix of feelings I'd never felt before rose up inside me.

'I love you, Violet,' I blurted. There was a silence.

'I love you too, dear girl,' she said eventually, an unusual tremble in her voice. 'I do hope Pearlbourne will be everything you imagined.'

All the groceries were still in the trolley under the stairs and the ice cream had started to melt. Everyone was going to think I'd been shoplifting. If anyone asked me, I was going to tell them I'd found a hundred euros on the ground.

I hung a bag on everyone's door. Toblerone and ice cream for Kitty. Sausages for Tony and Breda, and ice cream for Matt. The white pudding and teabags for Vlad, and the rest for me and Mam. I toasted the posh bread and buttered it. And while I was munching away, I set up an Amazon account, and ordered a Canon camera for Matt with a zoom lens and high quality nano-level pixel capacity, and I ordered a crate of champagne for Vlad. And a Blackrock Spa voucher for Mam, for back massages and facials and nails and reflexology and aromatherapy and loads of other things she deserved.

When I handed over the presents, I told everyone not to tell the others where they had come from. Like this was just my secret gift to them – that way I wouldn't have anything to explain. I ordered a Frisbee golf set and when it arrived, I secretly put the Frisbee baskets up in the back yard so Kitty had something to practise with. And when everyone wondered where they came from I shrugged my shoulders, saying maybe it's the rental company trying to improve the place. And no one asked any more questions after that. And Kitty was so delighted.

It was great to be able to buy stuff for people but I'd stretched it to the limit by then, because everyone was going to grow suspicious and I knew I had to stop. For the following weeks I did not sleep. I was constantly distracted. Every day I sprinted down the road to the cash machine to check the balance, and every day, the impossible number shone up at me, full of all its secrets and its promises. The truth is, although the money gave me so much hope, it frightened me too, and keeping it secret felt like a heavy burden, made me feel as if I was going a little bit mad. In my dreams I could see it, stacks and stacks of cash locked inside my bank account, but it was moving, like it was alive, rising and sinking like it was breathing.

Whenever I put my card in the machine, I began to think I could hear the money talking – but in a whisper that no one else could hear.

*

I found a company called DampFix Limited whose tagline was: 'Getting rid of Ireland's dampness: one patch at a time'. I told them I had a big job for them and explained about all the patches. I asked them for a quote and we agreed the price and fixed a date. Easy as that.

I hammered on Michael Graves's door. I knew he was in there. His radio was up loud and I could hear him coughing.

He opened the door. 'What the—'

'Don't say anything, Michael, please. I'm here with some instructions.'

He did his signature belly scratch and looked at me with his yellowed eyes.

'There is a repair company coming to The Flats next week. They are going to fix the damp problem. It's going to cost around ten thousand euros.'

He opened his mouth but I told him not to say anything until I'd finished talking and even though he didn't know I was rich, there was a power in me now, and he sensed it, I think, and did what he was told.

'Alternative accommodation arrangements have been made for all the residents. The whole thing will take a week. I will get a flyer printed up with information and distribute a copy to everyone in The Flats. Do you hear me? Do not answer any questions about the repair except to say it's all under control, and do not tell anyone you've been speaking to me about this. Everything has been paid for so it would be in your interests just to keep quiet and do as I say.'

If Michael Graves was amazed, he did his best to cover it up. He raised his chin in the air in a kind of nod.

'Do you know what people in school call us, me and Matt Crawford and Kitty O'Leary?' I continued. 'We're not called Penny, or Matt or Kitty any more. We're called smelly and stinky and rank because we can't get the smell out of our clothes. Did you know that? Do you even care?'

It didn't matter what Michael Graves knew or felt or cared about. I was fixing something and it was important and I couldn't hang about. There was lots more planning to be done.

Some people assumed Michael Graves was the one responsible for organising the damp repair, and he became much more popular. Breda and Tony, who normally hated him, started to say things like 'Hallooo, Mike!' or 'Well, Mikey boy!' and asking him how he was and thanking him for all he was doing for the place and he'd just nod his head silently.

I sent everyone vouchers for a week in a place called Parknasilla.

It was pure magic. On a strip of coastline with coves and beaches and jetties, and the bedrooms were white and the beds were huge and everything smelled like oranges and

162

roses. We all went: Me and Mam and Kitty and her mam and Matt and his grandparents. When we got there, Mam jumped up and down like she was a kid. Everyone swam in the swimming pool and got breakfast in bed and we played tennis and lounged around on soft chairs in the foyer and my mam looked so happy and young and all the lines on her face disappeared.

Matt's grandparents kept checking with the staff every time they had a meal. 'Are you sure we don't have to pay for this?' Tony would ask, and the waiter would say, 'Quite sure, sir. It's all covered,' just as I had instructed them. Even so, Matt's granddad stuffed money into the hands of the cleaners on the last day.

When we got back to The Flats the walls were fixed and the lights were working and there was a smell of fresh paint everywhere and a cleanness in the air that had never been in The Flats before.

'Someone must have threatened to sue them,' Breda figured as we all puffed up the stairs with the luggage. 'Otherwise it would have taken another hundred years for them to do anything about it.'

There were lots of other things I wanted to do straight away, but couldn't. I wanted to buy my mam a brand-new car, but how could this be explained? If I'd known Violet's deposit was going to happen, maybe I'd have been prepared to set more things in motion, but I wasn't money-ready.

I went to the Apple Store in the city and I bought a

brand-new laptop and a pink laptop bag and an iPhone. I hid them all under my bed.

Violet's money was not just the most generous gift of my life; it was proof that someone thought I was special. Proof I could have a new story. And every night I pulled my brand-new laptop from under my bed and checked for messages from Pearlbourne. And one night there it was. Even the Pearlbourne emails looked like magic, with a moving photo of a glowing pearl.

'Dear Penelope (pref Lola),' it said and I literally shivered with the thrill of it.

> We are delighted to confirm your place at Pearlbourne Academy for Exceptional Girls. We acknowledge that you previously applied for a scholarship and were unsuccessful, but please do not be in the slightest discouraged by this. Standard fee-paying students are selected according to different criteria, and we are very pleased now to welcome you in this capacity. We look forward to your arrival on August 31st. Attached are your reading lists, a map of the campus, and details of your uniform and equipment requirements.

There was a list of things I had to buy, and books I had to order, and there was a special shop in town that sold the Pearlbourne uniform. I could not breathe. I wanted to love every moment of looking forward to the new term and wished I couldn't feel this tight knot right at the centre of me.

And the whole time my head kept swimming with the million things I could now do.

Up until then, having no money had been part of who I was. Being poor leaked into everything: the things people said to me, the things I couldn't do, the way my teachers thought about me, the way I was treated, everything.

I was dazzled. Of course I was. I tried to think logically about it but the money did not give me logic. It released other things in me, like a crazy kind of generosity and the craving to fix a lot of things around me that were broken. It woke big fiery things I didn't even know had been burning inside me, like anger and rage and revenge and a kind of burning pride.

I got my hair and nails done in a salon, and bought a bucketful of make-up, and a literal wardrobe full of new clothes, and a new skateboard and I bought ten tickets for the Harry Styles concert and I went to Grace Grantham's house and I was wearing Gucci perfume and I called her on my new iPhone and said, 'Hey Grace, I'm outside your house and I've got something for you.'

And Grace came swaggering out and you could see she was amazed at the sight of me, the way her eyes went all round and the way she said, 'Wow'. And I handed her an envelope with the tickets in it and she said, 'Hey Penny, what's this?' and I said, 'See for yourself,' and after she

165

opened the envelope, she had to sit down on the wall, she was so shocked.

And I said, 'Sorry I'm so late with your present. You can bring all your friends or you can sell the tickets, I actually don't really care what you do with them.' She said she never meant to cut me off the way she did and she'd never meant the things she wrote in the note, and I said, 'It's OK, Grace, I get it.'

And she said, 'Will you come too?' and I said, 'Where?' and she said, 'To Harry Styles, with all of us. It would be great if you could,' and this is what I said to her then:

'If you and your poxy friends were the last people in the world, I still wouldn't go to the Harry Styles concert with any of you, or any concert, or anything at all. And even if I wanted to go, which I don't, I won't be around.'

'Where are you going?' asked Grace, a whole new expression on her face.

'I'm getting out of here. I'm going somewhere spectacular, away from Midgrey and away from this town and mainly away from you.'

'I'm sorry,' was all she said, holding the envelope tight to her chest.

And it shames me thinking about it now, how I walked off, how good it felt, how much I remember it still.

CHAPTER 15

A part from Violet, Millie Minton-Holmes was my only concrete link to Pearlbourne. I felt it was time to keep her in the loop. I phoned and talked to Connie, said I was back cleaning windows and asked her if she wanted me to drop round this weekend, and when she said, 'Yes, gosh, please do,' I asked if her daughter Millie would be around and I pretended my reason for asking was that I did not want to disturb her. 'As a matter of fact she will be home this weekend,' said Connie, 'but you can work around her.'

I arrived early. A blue plastic cover was still wobbling on the surface of the Minton-Holmes's swimming pool. Millie was stretched on the sun lounger in jeans and a t-shirt, shouting at Alexa for the song she wanted to hear. There was a deck chair beside her.

'Hello, Millie,' I said, sitting down.

'Eh, hello?' she said, propping herself on her elbows and then sitting up properly.

'Do you know who I am?' I asked.

'Em, you're the girl who cleans the windows?'

'Well, yes, but what I mean is, do you know my name?'

'No.'

'Good,' I said. 'I mean, . . . there are a few things I need to tell you.'

'Oh right,' she said, looking a bit quizzical. 'Do you need someone to help you with your buckets or something?'

'No. As a matter of fact I've forgotten some vital equipment so I'm afraid I won't be able to clean the windows today. Perhaps you'll tell your mother if I don't catch her. Send her my sincerest apologies about it. But since I'm here, I thought I might ask you some advice. I can't think of a better person.'

'Advice? What do you need advice about?'

'I understand you're a Pearlbournian.'

'Yes,' she said, rolling her eyes slightly, like she was a celebrity and I'd just asked her for an autograph. 'What do you want to know?'

'So, I'm starting in Pearlbourne this year and I wondered if you might tell me what to expect. It would be nice to get some advance info from someone who knows.'

'Sorry, what?'

'I'm going to Pearlbourne. This autumn.'

'You?'

'Yes, me.'

'Haha,' she said, combing her fingers through her hair

and rolling over on her side to look at me more closely. 'Very funny.'

'I'm serious.'

'You're not. Pearlbourne is not the kind of school for . . .'

'For who?'

'For, em, not trying to be mean or anything, but for people like you.'

'People like me? What do you mean?'

'People who clean windows for money. It wouldn't suit you. You couldn't afford it.'

'What about the people who win scholarships?'

'Oh, them. It's rather cruel really, those people are always such a terrible fit. They're always on their own. Fish out of water. So, now, stop playing with me and tell me what you really came here to say.' She smiled.

In one crashing wave, I understood completely. I understood, from the way she looked at me, from the way she sniffed, from the tight little smile on her face. I would never fit in if I came to Pearlbourne as I was.

'Gosh,' I said and tried to flash the same smile at her that she'd flashed at me. 'Golly, but I think you must be operating under some misapprehension.'

And a whole series of lies came blurting out so fluently and naturally that they didn't feel like lies at all. They felt like a new truth.

'When I'm out and about like this, I prefer to go by Penelope Nolan – but in actual fact, I am Lola Nolan-Fitzsimons. I'm the grand-niece of a woman you may have heard of. Her name is Violet Fitzsimons. My family is independently wealthy and we travel a great deal. My parents live abroad. When I'm here in Ireland, I live with my great aunt in Lavender House.'

'Oh. Wow. Very nice to meet you, Lola Nola-Fitzpatrick.'

'It's not Nola, it's Nolan,' I corrected. 'And it's not Fitzpatrick, it's Fitzsimons.'

I heard her rolling my new name inside her mouth, and I liked the sound of it.

'But seriously then, what's with the window-cleaning?' she asked. She rolled over on to her stomach then and was propping up her chin in her hands, waving her feet in the air.

'Oh sorry, have I not explained? I should have made that clear too. You see I like to do this for, em, for charity. It's a hobby of mine. I tend to get terribly bored when I'm here. All my friends are in Dubai and Greece and Monaco and Paris and Milan and New York and other such places. It's quiet here and I can't bear to sit around doing nothing. And before I get ready for Pearlbourne, this has been just as good a way to occupy my time as anything.'

It was like magic. Right in front of me, Millie swung her legs to one side and sat up. The neutral, borderline-snooty expression began to melt away. She looked so different then, her face all warm and open, her voice suddenly eager.

'Oh gosh,' she said. 'I literally had no idea! I mean I thought you were just here to clean the . . . I mean . . . and oh but this really is so marvellous. We hardly ever get new girls at Pearlbourne, other than the first years. And you are so . . . Wow. This is just great.'

'Yes, I'm thrilled about it too!' I replied. 'And since I'm only recently home from abroad and since I don't know anyone else who goes to Pearlbourne, that's the reason I thought of you. It would be brilliant if you could give me a steer – I need someone to show me the ropes. Tell me what to expect. Starting with the things I need to bring.'

'They should have sent you a list.'

'I have it.'

'Yeah, it's all on there.'

'I know, but I want to be sure I get the right stuff. Like it says a trunk, but I don't know what type is the best, and what brand of wash bag, and PJs, and stationery. It's not easy being the new girl and I don't want to get anything wrong.'

She told me she knew what I meant.

From Millie, I needed the code. I needed her to teach me my first lessons in how to be a Pearlbournian.

We ended up going shopping together. It turns out there is a Pearlbourne uniform for every possible occasion. Pearlbourne sweatpants, Pearlbourne shorts. Hockey sticks with the

171

Pearlbourne crest branded into it as if by hot metal. There are even Pearlbourne pyjamas. Palest pink silk, shining like mother of pearl, with the famous crest on the pocket.

'I want to hear ALL about you,' said Millie. 'Where have you been? What schools have you been in?'

'Have you heard of Sharjah International?'

'No.'

'Good,' I replied. 'What I mean is, most people haven't. It's quite exclusive. My parents value privacy above all else.'

'Of course they do. Well, look, honestly Lola, I couldn't be more chuffed. You coming to Pearlbourne is going to be the best thing ever.'

'Thanks for all the help,' I said. 'I couldn't be happier. I especially love my trunk. I'd never have known about it if it wasn't for you and I'd have arrived with all the wrong stuff and wheelie luggage. Now I can be pure class, just like you.'

'You're pure class anyway,' she said and then she hugged me tight. 'Have a splendid rest of the summer! Friend me on Facebook, will you?'

I told her I had zero social media presence and for a second she looked confused.

'No Instas? No Snapchat?' And I said no, nothing like that.

'OK right, well, see you at Pearlbourne. This is amazing.'

'Yeah,' I said. 'Amazing.'

She stood at the top of the stone steps at the front of the

Minton-Holmes's house and waved vigorously, and I waved back from the taxi and started humming the Pearlbourne song:

> 'Hearts of grit and hearts of fire,
> Never waa-aaver, never tire,
> Fly the Pearlbourne flag wi-ith pride,
> Truth and kindness doth a-abide.'

I had everything I needed. All I had to do now was transfer the fees, confirm my place, and sit the summer out.

After that, everything was tinged with pleasure. The football in the wild back yard. The noise of other people's business through the thin walls. My mother sleeping all day and working all night. Everything could be tolerated now.

And after a while the money didn't haunt me quite as much. It didn't whisper at me any more when I checked the balance at the machine. I stopped thinking about it as much as I first had.

I told Kitty and Matt the Pearlbourne scholarship was on again. I'd won it after all, I said. And I broke the news to Mam and told her how this was the best opportunity any human being could be given.

'But who? Where? How did you?'

173

It didn't take long to get her to believe me.

'Things seem to be turning around for us all,' said Mam, smiling a genuine, comfortable smile. 'You've got your scholarship. We've had such a wonderful break. The Flats have been repaired. The hallway even looks nice. Life is looking up!'

When she started fretting about all the stuff we'd have to buy, I told her she didn't have to worry about a thing. It was all covered.

'I'll call you all the time, and I'll be home every half term and holiday and you'll hardly even notice I'm gone,' I said.

'Do I have to come with you on the first day or anything?' she asked, twisting a tea towel around and around.

'No, there's nothing like that,' I said, knowing such a thing would terrify her. I couldn't tell her the truth. I couldn't tell her how glad I was to be leaving The Flats behind me.

Once I'd squared the whole thing with Mam, I began practising for Pearlbourne.

I pulled up all the posh school websites I'd pored over before, and listened to the tone of people's voices. I stretched out my vowels and tightened up my consonants and listened to the words they used and tried out the things they said, hearing how these new words sounded coming out of my own mouth. I spent entire nights playing clips of people talking. And I started mixing a few new words and phrases into my language: 'totally' and 'goodness' and 'gosh' and 'OMG' and 'amazing' and 'literally fab'.

I spent careful time looking at what boarding school people wore, how they did their hair, what shoes they walked around in, the kinds of bags they carried.

For the rest of the summer I built around myself a whole new history, like an armour – making me feel more like Lola Nolan-Fitzsimons and less like Penny Nolan. I dreamed of luminous green lawns, and old towers with the sweet sound of bells ringing out from inside them, and well-kept staircases, and polished wood, and teachers with unfrowning faces who said things like, 'We take every student for every minute and we focus on making them the best they can be.'

The day I first saw Millie Minton-Holmes, she'd been so perfect and remote, and she smelled of a world I thought I would never know – as if she'd been cleaned by a breeze of cut grass and peppermint. I kept remembering how when I'd found out she was a Pearlbournian I'd stared at my bitten nails and at the frayed ends of my jumper, thinking that so many wonderful things in the world were beyond me.

Now they were not beyond me. Now they were there for the taking.

My friends and I used to believe Violet was a terrible monster with glinting eyes and meat hook hands, but actually she had been my rescuer. I wished she was still next door. There was so much I wanted to say to her and

175

ask her. I kept wondering what had made her leave in such a hurry.

All through that summer, I became a professional online shopper – an expert in eBay orders. I tried to be careful not to make people suspicious. If they wondered about me, they didn't say – at least not directly.

'I wish I was lucky enough to find a load of money on the floor. That kind of thing never happens to me,' was all Kitty said about the matter.

Matt kept telling me how different I had started to look. 'Different, but still lovely,' he said one day. I told them I was getting ready for Pearlbourne, trying to become more interesting, more special.

'You were already good enough for us,' said Matt.

With the help of my new hairdresser, my scraggly lank hair was converted into a premeditated casual knot, just like Millie's. I made an effort to sit up straighter, to walk into a room with pride and poise. I arranged tendrils of hair in careful wisps, and checked the mirror, and put on jeans I'd ordered and a white linen shirt and my feet never felt more lovely in the expensive shoes I was now able to buy.

I knew the names of twenty-seven boarding schools around the world and had studied everything about Sharjah, where the students have bodyguards and there is a wall of privacy and protection, and hardly any social media presence because of the constant hazard of kidnapping.

If I was going to lie about myself I was going to do it properly. It was important to choose a history that could not easily be verified or checked.

'If there was ever a time for reinventing myself, it's now,' I told Kitty, who did not like the new me.

'Something's going on with her,' I heard my mam say on the phone one night to my Aunt Allie. 'She's changed. I'm not sure I like her new mood. Sassy's the word I'd use. Not like herself at all.'

I listened to her talking in the dark.

Not being myself. Being someone different. That was exactly what I was aiming for.

'Result,' I thought, closing my eyes and diving back into my recurring dreams of gymkhanas and rowing, house rules and prizewinning, bell-ringing and midnight feasts, horse-riding and hockey and Latin, homesickness and dress codes, curtseying and debating. Music rooms and music practice and music lessons and music recital and . . . music concerts. And dreams of me playing hundreds and thousands of perfect notes on a perfect piano.

By the time the summer was over, I'd completed my list. I ticked off the items as I laid them out on my bed: my uniform for class, my uniform for sport, my one-pieces for rowing, shoes for indoors, shoes for outdoors, good blazer, three jumpers, five shirts and the required supply of underwear and socks. A pack of five silver fountain pens. Books for all my subjects, and other books that looked interesting to me seeing as I could buy things now just because I felt like it.

We had to bring a small wash bag with essentials for the first night: nightwear, toothbrush, soap. My wash bag was Gucci, and the soap was Jo Malone, and my nightwear was going to be the same as everyone else's – shell-pink silk with satin borders, and slippers with the Pearlbourne oyster crest on each instep.

None of them would know I was a girl from The Flats. Part of me was already beginning to forget this too.

I booked a driver from a company I found online. I gave Lavender House as my address and told my mam and my friends the taxi was going to pick me up outside and there was no need to see me off. Mam said she'd prefer not to come downstairs so we said goodbye in the flat, which was fine by me. Matt came to the door to help with my trunk.

'Can't believe you're actually doing this,' he said, and I think his eyes were a little bit red which is the closest he'd ever got to crying in all the time I'd known him.

'Text us every day,' said Kitty. I promised I would and she hugged me so tight that I nearly choked. Of course I would stay in touch. They were my two best friends in the world. And anyway, I'd be back for a lot of the weekends and at half term so this wasn't really goodbye.

'From Blackrock to Pearlbourne Academy?' the driver

clarified as I climbed into the cool air of the biggest car I'd ever seen. I waved and smiled at Matt and Kitty and as I looked back at them through the rear window, I could see Matt blowing me an exaggerated kiss.

'Are you aware of how far away it is?' the driver continued.

'I am. Yes, I am,' I replied.

CHAPTER 16

The seat of this car was white leather. It squeaked when I shifted on it. I opened a cabinet door in front of me – all swirling, shiny wood. Tiny bottles of sparkling water with Oscar Wilde's face on their shimmering labels rattled in a silver rack. Chocolates sprinkled with crumbly toppings of blue and green and cream and purple and gold sat in clusters in two leaf-green enamel bowls.

'Help yourself!' said the driver. Normally free sweets would have been the thrill of my life. I'd have grabbed them by the fistful, but I could not eat. I was barely able to breathe. There was a plate of freshly sliced lemon wedges and a fat silver container with a round handle on top, tongs hooked on to the side. The container was for cubes of ice and from them, a little mist was rising. I picked a cut-glass tumbler from its shelf, clinked in two cubes using the tongs and poured the water. A sparkly fizz rose up.

I sipped and stared out at the blurred, speeding world that was going to look forever different to me now.

They say people are often disappointed when they come face to face with places they've dreamed about and longed for, but for me it was the opposite. 'Keep it together,' I whispered, because I could feel the blood in my veins and a *whoosh* inside my head.

I'd studied the Pearlbourne archway a hundred times, and for so long never dreamed this moment could be possible. Now those famous words were glittering in front of me. Now I could reach out and touch them.

WELCOME PEARLBOURNIANS. It didn't just mean other girls whose lives I would only read about in magazines or newspapers or websites of the rich. It wasn't just for people who were only ever going to brush past me, in a supermarket or on a street, all fragrant and wealthy and unaware. I was going to be one of those people. I was going to be a Pearlbourne girl. It was happening. Violet Fitzsimons had rescued me from a miserable, mediocre life and from now on I was going to be special.

'Are you all right, miss?' my driver said. His voice was very soft and there were layers of kindness in it. 'Is this your first term? Don't worry, you'll settle in in no time. Everyone does.'

'Thanks,' I replied, sniffing, letting him think I needed

to be comforted in this way. I pulled a tissue from its box and wiped away my tears of joy.

We crunched up the driveway. I pressed the button by the door handle and the window glided open. An exciting shiver of late-summer breeze blew in my face. On either side of me, strong, tall trees rustled and waved.

We reached the crest of a rising hill, and there was the building in all its perfection. The domed doorway, the glittering roof, the luminous lawns and the huge flag, flapping like it was greeting me.

To the right, a stone-blue bank of river. To the left, the swish and crackle of deep bottle-green forest with pathways leading into it from different directions, and beside the forest, an inlet of twinkling water and a colourful wooden boat house. The whole place was huger and wider than I had imagined and all of a sudden I felt smaller than I'd ever felt.

'Miss, this is it, we're here,' my driver said.

He opened my door and I stepped out into the light.

'Hello, Daly!' he said, shaking hands with a man who had appeared, pushing a brass trolley by its bars.

'Welcome, welcome!' said Daly. The driver took my trunk from the boot and Daly pleasantly wrestled it off him. 'I'll bring all this up to your dorm.'

After he'd arranged my luggage on his trolley, he took off his glasses and stepped back. 'Goodness, but this is one of the new faces, and you're taller than the usual new girls, so you must be . . . Wait, don't tell me!' He flipped through the pages of a clipboard hanging from the trolley rack, and peered at it, then took a more deliberate look at me. 'You must be Miss Nolan-Fitzsimons? Penelope – prefers Lola – Nolan-Fitzsimons,' he read.

'That's me.'

'Excellent! Delighted!'

We shook hands. I hadn't heard the driver starting up the engine again until the car began to reverse and turn around. 'Wait!' I shouted after him. 'Hold on,' I said to Daly, and ran towards the car. 'Sorry, hello, what do I owe you?'

The driver propped his elbow out of the open window and held his hand between us as if I'd said something rude or insulting.

'No, no, miss. It's all on your Pearlbourne account. You just need to sign.'

He handed me a wireless clicking machine. A receipt came rolling out. He tore it off with a flourish, smoothed it out on a small blackboard and handed it to me with a pen.

Four hundred and thirty-nine euros, said the receipt. There were times when I forgot about the money I had and this was one of those moments. I thought I would faint right there until I remembered again. While signing the receipt, I pictured what that much money would look like in notes, sitting on the counter at home, or stuffed into Mam's money jar. A rush of shame went through me then and

I had to keep myself from stumbling under the weight of it.

This was no time for feeling guilty. There was too much I needed to focus on, so I gulped and handed back the board and said goodbye.

The driver smiled. Wished me luck. Zoomed away.

Daly had disappeared by then and all my stuff with him, and I stood alone looking around, wondering where I was supposed to be. I'd been early on purpose. I thought it would put me at an advantage, but now I wished I'd waited until there was more of a crowd, so I could follow it and not feel so suddenly empty and directionless.

I walked, slow and unsure, around the huge turreted building. On the other side, there were more enormous grounds and a different driveway coming up out of the forest. Two women in jodhpurs and crested riding hats were directing a long queue of Range Rovers. Many of them were towing big trailers with horses inside.

'Horses to the left, please!' shouted one of the women, pointing urgently at the drivers.

Girls in sweatpants and Pearlbourne hoodies wandered randomly by. Some looked vaguely in my direction. Most of them didn't look at me at all.

On the front lawn were long, narrow outdoor tables covered in white linen tablecloths, piled with folded napkins and oval dishes full of miniature apple tarts. The

184

tarts were the size of small coins, and they had microscopic lattices on top and tiny dots of custard.

A group of girls nearby, all of them very thin, glared at the tarts like they were toxic. 'I'd say at least seventy-five apiece,' said one. It took a bit more overhearing before I realised they were talking about calories.

'Balls!' said another. 'Those things are a hundred per cent carb. I mean honestly, could they not put out some carrot sticks for once? Or apple slices? Or rice cakes and nut butter at the very least.'

'Here we go again,' said the first. 'I'll weigh a blooming ton by Christmas.'

Right then my hunger caught up with me and I thought I might starve to an immediate death so I shovelled about fifteen of the tarts into my mouth in one go, trying to be subtle about it. A couple of the girls looked over in my direction and then they seemed to whisper something to the rest of the group and then everyone stared. I stopped munching, just holding the pastries in my mouth, but there were flakes of pastry on my jumper. A little bit of laughter tinkled up into the air, and I wished I could run away.

The sleek, silent cars kept coming, swishing one after the other – and men in suits with polished pointy shoes got out of the driver's sides while slim women with perfect hair and pale fine-wool jumpers draped over their shoulders got out of the passenger's sides and everyone shook hands with everyone else.

Pearlbourne parents. I thought about Mam in her overalls and her rusty car and I swallowed down a great pang-swell of love and sadness and told myself not to think about her in case I lost my nerve.

'Hello!' Someone very tall was approaching me, holding out a hand. A huge glossy brown plait snaked over her shoulder, tied with a butterfly scrunchie. 'Allegra. Allegra Queensbury.'

'Penny – I mean Lola – Lola Nolan-Fitzsimons,' I stuttered.

'Is that your final answer?' she said. Her eyes narrowed for a second, and there was something hard about those eyes, I thought. But then she smiled.

'Sorry,' I said, trying to smile back. 'I was just thinking of someone else there for a sec.' I shook her hand and wondered for the first time ever whether the grip of a handshake can be too tight or too loose and whether there was a way to find out without having to ask.

'You the new third year?' she said, shielding her eyes from the sun.

'Yes,' I said.

'Fab, cool,' she said.

A loud bell rang then, and a booming voice rose above the noise. 'ATTENTION: ALL STUDENTS PLEASE ASSEMBLE FOR THE WELCOME SESSION.'

186

Allegra didn't show me where to go, and I didn't have a chance to ask because before I could say anything else, she ran off. There was something else in this cloud of exhilaration and amazement and I couldn't name it then but now, looking back, I know it was fear.

Fears are not all the same. They come in many varieties. Each has its own taste. Fear of being new tastes a bit like plastic. Fear of being different is bitter, like a lemon or a gone-off yoghurt. Fear of being found out is sour, like too much vinegar on chips. You might be able to ignore fearful thoughts but you can't ignore the way they taste.

I looked at these girls all chatting easily to each other and seeming as if nothing had ever worried them in their entire lives.

'What was I thinking?' I texted Matt.

'Are you there? What's it like?' he texted back immediately. 'And what u mean?'

'I don't belong here.'

'Then come home,' he said, but I knew I couldn't do that either. Not after all the trouble I'd gone to. Not after all the longing and wishing.

'I'll give it a try for a while,' I told him.

'OK, well good luck,' he said. 'You know where I am if you need me.'

A big shout of 'Oooooooh, look!' made me jump, practically dropping my mobile. 'Girl on phone outside phone hour! Who is this rebel we see before us?'

I looked up, shoving the phone into my pocket. Two more Pearlbournians striding up the incline were coming straight for me.

'I'm Lola Nolan-Fitzsimons,' I told them but they ran past like they didn't hear because now they were screaming in sudden reunion with another bunch of girls. 'Lily! Poppy! Mella! Shan!' they shouted, skidding violently into each other as I shrank away.

I was going to have to concentrate. Soak it up, drink it in, listen, and watch. My job for the days in front of me was to draw the history and rituals of Pearlbourne up from the ground through my feet.

Slowly, girls wandered down towards the domed doorway and the ringing bell. More girls with tanned legs and sun-bleached hair. More shrieking and hugging in clusters. More jumping up and down.

I was going to have to work hard to make sure no one here would see any evidence of the tense and anxious tangle at the centre of me. They would not discover the blanket of freshly-baked lies – already complicated and huge – I was going to wrap around myself to shield the real me from these Pearlbournians and their brightness and confidence and air of untroubled freedom. I was never going to be like them. The closest I was ever going to get was to pretend.

I felt as alone as I had during those nights in the dim hallway of The Flats when I had gazed at the Pearlbourne website, soaking up the details from my dark and secret distance. The doubts pinned me down and every breath I took was full of worry that this crazy plan would fall apart, my dream would evaporate and even with all the money in the world, I would still be lost.

Suddenly, I heard the putter and spit of a microphone getting plugged in.

'Testing, testing, one two three, can you all hear me?' It was Lucina Lucas, the head teacher. 'Hello, parents and hello, new girls and welcome back to our returning Pearlbournians!'

There was a ripple of applause, some muted whoops.

'Will all our first years please come up to the front where we can see you? Soon it will be time to go inside.'

Smaller, quieter girls, stunned and uncertain like me, filed to the front, socks fully up to their knees, shirts tucked in, hair pulled back into neat swinging ponytails.

'Oh, hello all of you.' She gazed down at them with an expression on her face that looked startlingly like love. 'I cannot tell you how wonderful it is to welcome you here. It is our job to make your first days at Pearlbourne as easy as they can possibly be. It will take some adjustment but soon you'll get the hang of it and we know your journey through Pearlbourne will be a memorable and happy one. So now!'

Lucina Lucas held her arms in the air like the statue of James Larkin on O'Connell St.

'I will be announcing the twenty-minute limit after which the school bell will ring again and this will be the signal. You must immediately say goodbye to your parents and let them be on their way.'

There was a good-humoured cheer from the adults at the back and a knowing look in their direction from Miss Lucas.

'We thank you for entrusting your girls to us, and, sorry, hush, please everyone, quieten down! There will be plenty of time later on to catch up on the shenanigans.'

Miss Lucas talked for a while more then about new beginnings and old traditions, about how everyone here belonged to a big Pearlbourne family and how the wall of girls had names on it dating back hundreds of years and how it connected us to something bigger and more ancient.

'You are all leaves on the same Pearlbourne tree, all stars in the same Pearlbourne sky, all flowers in the same Pearlbourne meadow.'

I looked into Lucina Lucas's eyes. It was like a meditation and it calmed me right down. I was kind of mesmerised, until a voice whispered close by:

'Jesus! It's the same every year. Is she ever going to shut up?'

A few people around me laughed and snorted, and when I turned to look at them they did not look back at me.

A wind was whipping up from the river. The leaves trembled and rustled from the forest and the twinkling water from the inlet by the wooden boat house had turned grey and choppy. Miss Lucas clapped her hands together.

'Right, now, remember what I said. Farewell to your parents and then all girls, inside! You know the procedure. Unpacking must be done without delay. Keep to your spaces and remember the dorms are not to be strewn with every scrap of every item you own. Put things in their places. Begin as you mean to proceed. Your dorm heads will be coming around to check that everything's shipshape. Supper in the ref no later than six-thirty p.m. and then, as long as everyone does as they are bidden, welcome cocoa and marshmallows in the games room.' This announcement got a massive cheer. 'Make sure you arrive for supper ready for bed. I'm talking PJs, I'm talking slippers, I'm talking dressing gowns.'

Three girls with violins stood up in the seated crowd and began to play, and my heart flipped over, and then everyone rose together as if they were one, and the bell rang out again and the grass on the hills seemed to lean towards the music. Hundreds of girls found their parents again to kiss their cheeks and to wave and then they began to move inside, single file, and all I could do was stand there and stare and then follow. Millie was two years ahead of me, and had already warned me that we mightn't cross paths for a while. I scanned and searched but didn't find her.

A woman in flat shoes and a tweed skirt was marching along the line.

'Right then, on we go!' she boomed at first and then, 'Could Penelope Nolan-Fitzsimons please make herself known to me if she is on campus. Penelope Nolan-Fitzsimons, please. Miss Nolan-Fitzsimons.'

I put my hand up and she came up close, smiling and saying, 'Hurrah, you are here. No queue for you! This way, my dear.'

She told me she was Mrs Halloran, my dorm head, and jostled me to the top of the line. 'I prefer Lola,' I said, and she said, 'Good, I'm so glad. Penelope would have been a terrible mouthful.' I followed her in through the entrance and along a red-carpeted corridor and through an oak door with big studs and a wide circular ring for a handle.

'Here are your roommates.' Three girls were sunk into huge armchairs, half sitting, half lying. One of them I already knew: Allegra, who'd shaken my hand earlier and run off. The other two struggled out of the comfy chairs, then walked towards me smiling. 'This is Jane,' Mrs Halloran said, as Jane hugged me, 'and this is Quin.' Quin shook my hand (so many handshakes!). Allegra got up more slowly and ambled over eventually. 'Lola, meet Allegra,' said Mrs Halloran and Allegra tipped her chin up ever so slightly and looked at me in that confusing way she had looked at me before.

'Hello, hello!' said Jane. 'You're the first new PB'er we've had here since we started! Love your name. I've never met a Lola. It's brilliant to meet you.'

'Hello,' I said, 'thank you,' which didn't come anywhere close to how grateful and relieved I actually felt because I could tell already she was lovely, the way you often can with people who are properly decent.

Still, the fear was not going away. It didn't help that they stood in front of me in a row, all open-faced and full of expectations I didn't think I'd ever be able to meet.

The second girl, Quin, was small and neat, her feet planted apart. Her handshake had been strong and long-lasting and I could still feel its imprint after she'd finished. 'Quin's the name! How do you do?'

'I'm well, thank you.'

Was my voice too quiet? Did I seem too timid? Was I speaking right?

'Hello, we met already on the lawn,' said Allegra and I wondered why she hadn't told me then that she and I were going to be roommates, because she must have known.

'Hi again, Allegra,' I said, still hoping the whole time I wasn't going to slip up or reveal myself or say anything out of place.

'We're your dorm sisters!' said Quin.

'Your roomies!' said Jane.

'It's our job to show you the ropes!' said Allegra.

'Yes, indeed,' said Mrs Halloran. 'These three have a special responsibility for getting you into the swing of things, and if I may say so, you couldn't be in better hands.'

'Our dorm will be a squash now you're here,' Allegra said. To anyone else it might have seemed like she was looking straight at me, but actually she was staring past me at some distant thing. 'Hope you don't have too much stuff. Hope you're not messy.'

'Don't mind her,' said Quin. 'Allegra likes things the way she likes them.'

'What's wrong with that?' said Allegra and maybe I was imagining it, but I thought I could see the slight flash of a sneer in her face.

'It's just been the three of us since first year,' said Jane, 'and we're so glad to have you.'

'But it's, you know, a fourth in our dorm,' Allegra piped up again. 'Well, it's going to take some getting used to.'

'But we're thrilled you're here, aren't we?' said Quin, and Jane said yes of course they were, and Allegra said nothing at all.

After Mrs Halloran left, I thought about texting Matt again and also Kitty, but I was under pressure time-wise because I had to change into my new Pearlbourne PJs and there were loads more people to be introduced to, and I was going to have to devote the rest of the evening to getting to know my dorm sisters better. Things had started well, but I couldn't be complacent, especially after Jane said: 'By the time we go to sleep I plan to know you as well as we know each other.'

'Challenge accepted,' I said, trying to sound light-hearted and casual. I think it worked because everyone laughed. I was so relieved and exhausted that I wouldn't have minded going straight to bed then, but again the bell rang and they jumped.

As we hurried along the shiny corridors towards the 'ref', they told me about the teachers who were decent and the ones who could be mean and who to make friends with and who were 'downright shockers', and the kinds of things you could get away with and the kinds of things you could not.

And all the time I could hear the buzz and clink of the refectory getting louder and louder, and just before we went in, Allegra slid her arm into mine and the fastness of my pulse got faster still.

'Remember, we want to learn ALL about you tonight, so don't fill up on too much food and then drop into a carb coma as soon as we go to bed. There's a lot of content to cover before anyone sleeps.'

And she let go of my arm and it felt like her words had contained some unseen threat, and the crowd swirled around me and there was a whirl of dream noise. The feeling of suddenly being cut off from the world outside. The padding of school slippers on polished floor. The smell of tea and cake and plates of bread and butter, and special cocoa in honour of 'first night back' made from hot foaming milk, with lollipops of real chocolate for dipping in and stirring around and tiny cubes of marshmallow bobbing around on top.

And somewhere in the middle of it all, I lost my nerve and knew I would not be able to construct and explain my new identity, nor reveal my old one. I felt silenced and trapped and was gripped with a massive urge to grab some of my most essential things and run away from Pearlbourne.

By the time we got back to the dorm, Allegra, Quin and Jane were in a tangle of summer catch-up. 'Florida is such a bore,' said Allegra.

'The Seychelles was brilliant,' said Jane.

'Aix-en-Provence would have been better if my brothers hadn't all showed up with their girlfriends,' said Quin. And then they went on a bit more about the people they had met and the places they had gone and the things they had done.

I knew that soon they'd be asking me all kinds of questions about my own summer and my skin felt numb and my brain was tired from all the colour and sound and from knowing it would have to keep track of all the lies I was preparing to tell. It felt like I was carrying hidden weights chained on to me under my brand-new Pearlbourne PJs.

Here it comes, I thought as their faces turned towards me.

'Right!' Allegra threw herself on her bunk, lay on her back and put her hands behind her head. 'Let's begin. Parents' names please.'

'What?' I said.

'Who are your parents? What are their names?' She spoke slowly, like I was a little kid.

'Why do you want to know that?' I said.

'Just tell us their names, that would be a start,' said Allegra. I could see Jane glaring at her as she settled into her own bunk, and I climbed the ladder to mine and asked Allegra again why she wanted to know the names of my parents.

'You can trust us, you know,' she said.

'What makes you think I don't trust you?' I whispered back, a little shocked.

'Many things,' she replied. 'Like how you won't look me in the eye.'

My mouth felt suddenly dry and muffled. 'Like how you're so cagey about yourself.'

'I'm not cagey. I'll tell you whatever you want to know.' There was nothing I could do to control the high-pitched reediness that was creeping into my voice.

'Look,' sighed Allegra. 'I get it. But there's nothing to worry about. There are at least seventeen students here who are a permanent kidnap risk. You're no more important than any of us. You should be careful not to act as if you are.'

'I'm sorry, Allegra, I didn't mean . . .' Already everything felt off-kilter.

Allegra got out of her bunk and marched over to the door, waiting by the light switch. 'I can hear Halloran on the corridor,' she said. 'Get under the covers!' Everyone did, and Allegra turned off the light.

There was a short silence as I stared into the darkness, waiting for my eyes to adapt, and then the door clicked open, and Mrs Halloran said, 'Excellent, good night,' and the door closed again and some whispering began and I thought I heard a choked laugh and then I definitely heard Jane saying, 'Shut up, the two of you, honestly.'

If this was my Pearlbourne dream, it wasn't coming true the way I had expected. Allegra was right about me not being more important than anyone else, but still I thought, I had a right to be here. I was committed now, and I was going to make the most of it. I was going to breathe in every atom, and I was going to feel grateful and happy for all the things the rest of them probably took for granted. I was going to do my best not to worry if Allegra and Quin's whispers were about me, and whether it was me they were laughing at.

'Lola. Hello, Lola. Are you still awake?' came Allegra's voice, then, 'We've so much more to ask you about.'

'Oh, stop being such a bully,' said Jane as I decided the only thing to do now was pretend to be asleep. 'You know, maybe, just maybe, she doesn't feel like telling you all about herself. Maybe you've made her feel uncomfortable. It can't be easy to have to fall in with all of us at the beginning of third year. Leave her alone for a while, Allegra, will you? Let her get to know us all a bit better first before starting your interrogation.'

I could hear Allegra giggling and mumbling something else. As I lay silently in the dark, my fists were so tight that I ended up digging little half-moon marks into the palms of my hands with my nails. I was sure they would hear the sound of my clattering heart so I lay on my stomach and pressed my chest to the mattress to silence it and concentrated hard to stop my breathing from becoming ragged and quick and I imagined this night would be a restless and tormented one.

But in the end I fell into a sleep so deep and so heavy that it seemed as if only a moment passed before I could hear the squawking of birds and the shriek and rattle of an old tap turning on, and the ringing of the morning bell.

CHAPTER 17

I was going to do my best to stay out of everyone's way. But when Jane was in the shower and Quin was drying her hair, Allegra cornered me.

'Gosh, Lola, you should really have been gone by now,' she said, looking at the bleeping face of her Apple Watch.

'Gone where?'

'Your lake run.'

'My what?'

'Did nobody tell you? It's an ancient Pearlbourne tradition. Old Halloran should have briefed you last night, but she must have forgotten.'

Allegra pulled a nail file from her wash bag and began filing her nails.

'On everyone's first morning here, they're supposed to do a run around the lake and submit their times. It achieves two objectives. It gives newcomers more of a measure of the place. Helps them get their bearings, so to speak, and secondly, if you submit a good time there's the added bonus of providing an early signal for the athletic teaching team about any new talent they should be looking out for. The first years have probably all set out already. You need to get going.'

'Is that really a thing?' I asked.

'Is it a thing?' she asked, her voice full of controlled amazement. 'What do you mean, is it a thing? Lola, seriously, you really must stop being so wary of everyone here. It's not just a thing. It's compulsory and it's important. So come on, get your gear on, quick as you can. Put on your runners and start from this door, go out the main entrance and follow the lake around to the left by the shed, and come all the way around. Run fast as you can bear, it'll be worth it. I'll time you. You really better get a move on, or you'll miss first period. It's poetry and Miss Engels loses her sense of reason entirely if anyone's late. Come on, go go go!'

I did what she told me, and soon I was out in the early morning chill, listening to the sound of my own breathing and taking in the view. The run took me along a forest pathway and it made me relax a bit, and trust the process. This was a good tradition. It cleared my head and gave me some distance and Allegra was right, it was a good way of becoming familiar with the grounds and having a look around on my own terms. And I was picking up pace and grateful to Allegra for letting me know about this tradition that I might otherwise have missed out on.

My heart kept lifting because this was magical – a glimmering bridge and a little paved garden well tended in the middle of nowhere – and though I rushed past it all I was noticing details and managing to focus on my speed too, and I might even have made good time except for what I came across that made me stop, that took my breath away, that drew me to it like an ancient magnet.

It was just past a muddy part of the path, darkened by another patch of forest and difficult to see at first, but as I got closer to the broken gates and a crumbling moss-covered wall I became surer. I stopped worrying about my time and my speed, and instead I gazed at the functionless rusty chain that might once have held those gates closed. I clambered over them and into this old space, and there were the twisted frames of swings and a giant measured circle engraved into stone, clogged now with mud and leaves. I touched the swing frame and it creaked a little spookily, and I looked around at the ruins of what once was part of Violet's Pearlbourne adventure. This was the maths garden. A sparkling part of Violet's memory. Pity, I thought to myself, wandering around and hearing the music of Violet's voice in my head, remembering again that being here was her gift to me, and that I must try to cherish it.

I sat on a jagged edge of a roundabout and the rasping

rusty screech it made startled me and echoed a little in the air. After that, apart from the snaps and clicks of the forest wood, there was silence.

'Help me, Violet,' I said out loud. And just as I said that, high up and far away, the sound of the Pearlbourne bell rang out again, reminding me that I'd wrecked my lake run time, and would now be late for the very first class and it was poetry and there was a teacher called Miss Engels and apparently she would lose her sense of reason.

It took me twenty minutes to run back to the school, and then another ten to find where the classroom was, and when I came through the door they all looked at me and some of them frowned and some of them laughed and some of them covered their mouths. I was the only one in PE gear. The rest of them were in their blazers and their hair was all washed and brushed and styled. Miss Engels was a brittle-looking woman of about seventy and when she saw me coming through the door, her lips turned from pale pink to blue. I was covered in mud from my knees down, and every step I took towards the empty desk was accompanied by squelching noises and left a mucky footprint on the parquet floor.

'Who is this?' she said, as if she could not bear to speak directly to me.

'This is the new third year!' It was Allegra, sitting at the back, smiling broad and innocent. 'Her name's Lola.'

Miss Engels sat down as if the shock of my arrival had

somehow weakened her. 'Lola, why is it that you are so late that class is nearly over?'

'Em, I'm sorry, I was doing my run around the lake.'

'Your what?'

Miss Engels looked down at a list on her desk.

'Lola. Penelope Nolan-Fitzsimons. Please may I ask you what in heaven's name prompted you to run around Pearlbourne lake this morning?'

'My newcomer's lake run,' I said, looking towards the back of the class where Allegra slowly drew a finger across her own neck, staring at me. 'I mean, I was just . . .' I continued, realising with a dizzy, sudden bolt of shock that I had been tricked. 'Em, I don't know,' I said. 'I just felt like going for a run and then I got sort of, em, waylaid. I'm really sorry.'

'And what, furthermore, possessed you to arrive to class in such a disordered state? Where is your uniform? Where are your books?'

'They're in my trunk in my dorm.'

I could see Quin looking confused, and Jane glaring at Allegra, and a blur of eyes all looking in my direction.

Miss Engels told me to leave and get myself 'sorted out' and never to come to class late in such a condition again. And the heat of my humiliation burned so fiercely inside me that as I reversed out of my chair and hurried from the room, it felt as if steam was rising from me through my clothes.

In the corridor I had to ask directions from Daly, and I didn't even say thank you when he gave them to me, and I ignored him when he shouted after me, 'Miss, miss, do you need any assistance?' and just ran and ran to the refuge of the empty dorm.

I sat on the low pink chair beside the sink and stared down at my muddy shoes and my Pearlbourne socks smeared with blackened slime. I clamped my teeth together and white sparks appeared at the edges of my vision and I raged inside my head about the lies that Violet had told. How she had promised that Pearlbourne was going to be perfect and lovely. How many friends for life I was going to make. How nurturing and loving the teachers were. How there would never be a moment of anything but engagement and joy and the best kind of learning.

I remembered my mam's bitter words that at the time I had not listened to: 'Anyone who tells you their school days were perfectly happy, well they're either lying to you or they're lying to themselves,' and I began to realise that she might have been right. The only other explanation was that Pearlbourne had changed. If once it had been the perfect place of Violet's memories, it wasn't that any more. The maths garden had fallen into disrepair and there were mean girls everywhere waiting to deceive and dominate and who knows what they'd do if they found out any of my secrets. I wished I was not weak and fragile. I was supposed to have been strengthened by Violet's money, but I was worthless, I realised. Nothing had changed for me. Maybe nothing was ever going to.

I tried to ring Violet then but the dial tone was strange and echoey and the recorded voice of a woman speaking in a language that I did not recognise told me that Violet was way beyond my reach now, that I was on my own and that no one could help me navigate the complications and secrets of how to survive, how to fit in, how to feel good about yourself in a place like this. It was only day one, and already Allegra had taken all my purpose away.

There was a knock on the door and I jumped and then dashed to open it. It was Mrs Halloran.

'What's happened? How are you getting on? I thought you were settling in well but I've just heard about your wild running and non-compliance and I have to say I am extremely concerned.'

She looked at my face and looked down at my feet and a shadow of realisation fell across her face.

'Somebody put you up to this, didn't they?' she said, but I would not answer. I just looked down at the ground. 'You don't have to say anything. I see it now so clearly. I should have known. It was Allegra, wasn't it? How malicious of her when you're just finding your feet.'

'Please, Mrs Halloran, please don't say anything to her. I'd rather try to handle Allegra by myself if you don't mind.'

Mrs Halloran's face softened and she sat on the bed beside me. She nodded her head silently for a while and then said, 'You know, I do think that is quite the wisest strategy. Navigate this hiccup under the radar. Yes, much the best thing. Let's keep this storm inside its teacup, shall we?'

And I said yes, and she urged me to get showered and to get on with the rest of my day in as ordered a way as I could manage. She peered into my eyes the way people at Pearlbourne often did in those early days, as if searching for the real story of me. Maybe there was no way out. I didn't want to stay at Pearlbourne but I couldn't bring myself to go home either. I felt battered already and didn't know what to do. For a whole day, I could not speak.

'Don't let her bully you like this,' Jane advised at lunch, knowing exactly what had gone on to make such a disaster of my first morning. 'Always check with me first when Allegra tells you anything. Anything at all. She's dreadful like that. You need to be on top of your game with her.'

But even though she was being nice, I couldn't say a word, not even to thank her. And Jane stopped talking as well, like she too had been made mute by the bubble of silence I had begun to surround myself with.

This whole idea had been a terrible plan, and I thought I was sunk. I didn't know then how quickly things can change at boarding school, and how rescuers can come at unexpected moments, and I didn't know that when we were all getting ready for bed that night, me locked in my silence and Allegra calling the shots with the other two, my rescuer would rock up with a knock on the door.

CHAPTER 18

It was more like a bang, and everyone stopped what they were doing. I was brushing my teeth by the sink. 'Let me in!' shrieked a voice outside and then a girl plunged into the room so shrill and squeaky that I didn't recognise her at first. 'Lola Nola!' she shouted, flinging her arms around me and jumping up and down so that I had to as well.

It was Millie Minton-Holmes.

I was thrown to see her acting like this compared to all the languid coolness I knew her for. She wrapped her arms around Quin and Jane too and threw herself down on Allegra's bunk.

'Move over,' she said, and Allegra did what she was told. 'Lola Nola's a friend of mine, understand? I've heard a rumour that someone is trying to get one over on her, and I won't have it, does everybody hear me?'

She got up again and linked arms with me and still I didn't know what to say.

'If anyone here tries to do anything to upset you, they'll have me to answer to,' she said and then let me go again and did the 'I'm watching you' sign to Allegra with her middle and index finger. 'Seriously, if I hear of anyone giving her a hard time, I'll plot the consequences – isn't that right, Lola Nola?

'Lola is from an important family, and she's connected to some very important people too, and you'd do well to be as nice to her as you possibly can, isn't that right, Lola?'

My three dorm sisters had stopped moving completely.

'Now Lola, I think it's time to tell them all about yourself, if you haven't already. It's OK. I'll make sure they keep anything confidential to themselves.'

Millie swept out of the room again and somehow my silence evaporated as I remembered that, of course, I'd already lied confidently to Millie, and somehow this reminder made me able to go through with it at last, to tell them my prepared story, to spin them my invented yarn.

'I am the grandniece of Violet Fitzsimons, and when I am in Ireland, I stay with her.'

'Where's that?'

'It's a place called Lavender House, in Blackrock, County Dublin.'

'Oh, oh yes, that's near Millie,' Quin said to the others. 'Lola's practically a neighbour of hers.'

'Yes, we know each other very well!' I said quite loudly, feeling slightly flushed and a bit elated. 'I've been to her house. We've spent loads of time together. I even know her mam.'

'Her mam?' said Allegra. 'Her *mam*?'

'Yes, her name is Connie.'

'Surely you mean her *mum*?' said Allegra.

'Yes, I mean mum, sorry I thought that's what I said. Anyway, Millie's been a brilliant help – getting me ready to come here – we went shopping together in July. She helped me pick out everything I brought here, even my trunk.'

'It's a lovely trunk, all right,' said Quin, running her fingers along the metal corners. 'So where were you before this?'

'Oh, you probably haven't heard of it. An international boarding school in Sharjah.'

'Wow,' they all said together.

'We love Millie. She's so lovely. We all love her. Don't we?' said Jane, filling the silence that followed.

'We so do,' said Quin, and Allegra nodded along.

'OK, good progress, so we know where you live and we know you have a great-aunt called Violet Fitzsimons. What about your parents?' asked Allegra.

'Dad's in oil. He's based in Dubai,' I said. 'And my mother works for the government and there's no point looking them up. For security reasons they've no social media presence. You won't find anything about them online.'

'OK, excellent, that'll do for now. Next question, where

do you holiday?' asked Allegra, and there was a tense moment when I had to ask her what that meant.

'You know, your holiday home? As in, France or Italy or Sydney or wherever.'

'Oh, right,' I said and scrabbled desperately around my brain for something to say – and when it occurred to me, I shouted 'GREECE!' so loudly that everyone laughed. 'Greece, yes. That's where my holiday house is.'

'Wow, Greece, fab. Oh, quite terrific. Very cool. Whereabouts?' asked Jane.

'On an island.'

'Wow, cooler still, ' said Quin. 'Which one?'

'Em, you've probably never heard of it. There are six thousand of them.'

'Just TELL us,' said Allegra.

'It's called Spetses,' I mumbled.

They all scrolled on their phones to google it. And before I'd even made a decision to, I was telling them the house was called Spiti Tou Kapetaniou.

'It means The Captain's House,' I explained, trying to roll my eyes in exactly the same way I'd once seen Millie rolling hers.

'And what's it like?' Allegra blinked slowly at me.

'It's OK. Quite comfy for a nineteenth-century traditional seafront mansion.'

'Oooooh,' said Quin.

'Nice. Very nice,' said Allegra.

They actually found the stupid house online and did these high-pitched shrieks and Jane said, 'Gosh Lola, that really does look DIVINE!'

It got nearer to lights out, and right then I felt like a pilot trying to land a plane in the dark when one of the engines had failed. But when the night bell rang Quin and Jane hugged me and said how thrilled they were to hear so much brilliant stuff about me and what a fascinating person I was and how they hadn't known what to make of my silence and my lack of communication but now that they were getting to know me, how great and interesting I was, and how lucky they were to have me in their dorm.

CHAPTER 19

When I woke the next day everyone was up. Jane pulled the gold rope, which whipped up the dorm's main window blind into a tight roll and threw white light into the room like it had been set on fire. Quin had a towel around her neck and was brushing her teeth at the sink and Allegra was fully dressed, standing in front of the long mirror by the wardrobe, slowly braiding her hair into its big plait.

'I'm very proud of you,' she said to me. I just looked at her.

'I mean, I hope you realise that little trick I played on you was just a test.'

'What kind of test?' I managed to reply, trying to be calm and trying to stay in control.

'A test of loyalty to your dorm sisters. I can now confirm that Lola Nola is no snitch, and in this way I've done a service to us all, by enabling you to prove yourself and by reassuring Quin and Jane here as to your bona fides.'

'Em, Allegra, we never asked you to be so mean to her. We already knew she was OK,' said Jane.

'Yes, well, always good to have these things confirmed,' replied Allegra, looking pleased with herself. 'What do you say, Lola?'

'I'm not sure what to say,' I said.

'OK, well let's leave it at that then, shall we?' she replied.

There were seven texts when I checked my phone. Six from Kitty. One from Matt, each of them asking me how things were going. 'All good,' I texted back, sitting up. 'Will send more news when I have time.'

There were no messages from Mam, but she had always been a terrible texter, and I wasn't going to be able to phone her that morning because I definitely didn't want to be late for anything.

The lines of students moving from the dorms towards assembly hall made this kind of rustling sound I'd never heard before, and it was a little like being caught up in a river. Everyone's teeth were straight and white and their hair was perfect and the sunlight bounced off them as if they were all made of gold. The girls all purred with wealth – I thought they glowed with an inner warmth of the certainty and happiness that being rich brings. And for the first time since I'd arrived,

I thought about the morning Midgrey mob and the jostling and the shouting and the insults thrown up and down the corridors. When the Midgrey principal spoke, no one could ever hear him on account of the uncontrollable baying noises coming from the student crowd. You were lucky to make it to your locker without suffering a minor injury.

When Miss Lucas spoke the room became pure and quiet, smooth and ordered. The line of girls swished past long windows and great paintings in silver frames and huge vases on the floor with blue and white flowers crowded into them.

Quin and Jane stayed close by and Allegra kept her distance.

That second morning just after assembly, a woman appeared out of the crowd whose face I also recognised from the website. Margot Barnard. She scanned the room and fixed her eyes on me and smiled, then walked in my direction. Putting her hand on my shoulder she said, 'Are you Penelope?' and I said yes but I preferred Lola, and she said, 'Very good. I've just been rereading your letter of recommendation from Violet Fitzsimons and remembering how very pleased I was to learn you would be joining the Pearlbourne family. I'm the music teacher.'

'I know,' I said.

'Which is to say it's my job to seek out and cherish musical talent. It's my vocation to hone emerging skills and help the gifted here to persist and be patient.' And in that moment I could already hear the thousands of notes I would play for her.

'I must tell you!' she continued. 'Violet Fitzsimons was my music teacher when I was your age. She is a wonderful woman. How is she? How is it you are her student too? I didn't even know she was still giving lessons!'

'Lola is her grandniece!' piped up Jane, all knowledgeable and proud.

'Really?' said Miss Barnard. 'Is she? My goodness! But I don't remember Violet mentioning that . . .'

'She didn't want to make a big deal of it. She decided it was better not to draw too much attention,' I stuttered.

'Of course, ah yes, I understand, quite right. Does not do to weigh a new student down with the unfair expectation of such an auspicious association or indeed to bestow any unfair advantage. And it is certainly quite a thing to be the grandniece of Violet Fitzsimons.'

'I know,' I said, wishing she would shut up about it now.

'Still, I must telephone her to tell her how happy I am to be teaching you this term.'

'You can't phone her. She's uncontactable. She's away right now in a very remote country and she's not coming back for ages,' I said in this quick blurty way I was starting to get used to.

217

Miss Barnard's eyebrows rose for a second and fell again.

'Oh, right – OK then, thank you,' she said. 'In any case, Lola, just to say again you are very welcome indeed.'

I was scarlet. I hoped they'd all assume it was just because I was still shy and new and they wouldn't see it for what it was – the embarrassment and panic that comes with being a fraud.

'I wouldn't have recognised you,' continued Miss Barnard. 'You look nothing like her.'

'Yes, I mean no,' I said stupidly. 'Like I say, I don't really like to go on about it.'

'No, of course, message received loud and clear.' She laughed a little nervous kind of laugh. 'Now, as soon as you're fully settled in I will send you our first scheduled consultation and then we shall decide on your music curriculum. Greatly looking forward to that!'

'Miss Barnard!' came a voice from across the hall, and she turned.

'Oh goodness, yes, Miss Lucas, coming straight away. I must dash, see you soon, cheerio!'

'What's a consultation?' I asked Jane.

'Oh, it's just a thing everyone does with Barney when they first come here. You have to choose a piece to play and she sits listening to you and then writes down all these details about what your current standard is.'

'OK,' I said.

'But it should be more or less a doddle for you, shouldn't

it?' said Allegra. 'Seeing as your great-aunt is a famous teacher and we've all heard you're like some sort of piano genius.'

'Genius? Where did you hear that? God no,' I mumbled, feeling another new pressure bearing down on me.

I thought about sneaking down to check out the music rooms and to run my fingers over the pianos. I thought it would be better to get my first look out of the way and in private, so I'd be less dazzled or stunned when I had to show up there for class. But it had been made clear to me after my first morning that there was no sneaking allowed and no opportunity for casual wandering at Pearlbourne. Time does not belong to anyone there.

The first chance I had to be in the music room didn't happen until the bell rang for Wednesday's music slot – the time of my scheduled consultation. I still didn't even know where the music wing was, and Jane had to show me how to get there. It was miles away from the day classrooms and we had to run, and I had to try very hard not to stop and stare at the corridors and passageways with the paintings and at the teachers and the flawless girls dashing in all directions. I could hear the strings room before I saw it, echoing with some screeches and some high notes and some low notes and the odd sweet note as people casually tuned up their instruments together.

'Here we are!' said Jane. 'Good luck with Barney. She's not bad, but her standards are high. She has no time for musical dunces like me. Kicked me out halfway through second year. Said I distinguished myself by making the piano sound like a baby elephant was dancing on the keys. Much too heavy-handed.' She shrugged. 'Hope it goes well for you though!'

The noise as I got close seemed harsh and vivid. The door opened like it had a mind of its own. A thousand times I'd been here in my head, and now I was stepping for the first time into the pale-blue-walled space, the pianos shining up at me and Miss Barnard in the middle of the room, twirling slowly around. Three girls were there already, sitting at pianos, doing scales at a superfast pace. They stopped and turned on their swivel stools, looking at me blankly.

Miss Barnard wore silk trousers and long white flared sleeves. I wondered how anyone at Midgrey might have reacted if they saw someone like her at the front of the class. They'd think somehow she'd wandered off the pages of a magazine or off a movie set, I reckoned. They'd freeze at the rise and fall of her lyrical voice.

'Welcome, Lola! Welcome to Pearlbourne piano room!' she announced.

It felt like I'd been welcomed over and over again since the day I'd arrived. By Wednesday, I'd begun to wish people would stop.

'Take your time,' Miss Barnard said. 'Get your bearings. Make yourself comfortable. It really is a wonderful space. We all take it so much for granted. Do have a look around. River facing! It allows, I often think, for a measure of wildness – always a good thing for musicians.'

I walked over to the huge, tall window and stood looking out. The river was ocean-rough and foamy, and a sudden rain shower seemed to be moving in from over the water. In less than a minute, a flash of raindrops whacked against the window as if someone had thrown a fistful of gravel at the glass, right in front of my face. I jumped and dropped my sheet music. Everyone gasped and asked if I was OK, and one of the girls rushed over to help me pick everything up.

'What piece have you chosen?' Miss Barnard asked. I held up the pages Violet had given me.

'It's the second movement of Beethoven's Sonata number eight,' I said.

'Very well, good choice, so be it. Now stop standing like a deer in headlights, and sit yourself down and let's be hearing you.'

'Thank you, Violet,' I remember saying very quietly and then immediately hoping I hadn't said it out loud and burning with another sudden blush.

'I don't know what my, em, my great-aunt has told you, but I'm not very good. I still have a lot to learn,' I said.

'Now, now,' Miss Barnard laughed, 'let me be the judge

of that. Why don't you take a place at the Bösendorfer. Or would you rather one of the Steinways?'

I'd no idea what those words meant and stood there cluelessly as everyone kept staring at me. There was something about the low-level nark in their faces that just for a moment reminded me of Grace Grantham and her friends.

I figured out Miss Barnard was talking about the names of the pianos. I sat at the one she'd said was a Bösendorfer and she said, 'Excellent choice'.

'We're just doing some simple scales right now as a warm-up,' shouted Miss Barnard as the girls struck up their practice again. 'Then we'll give everyone a turn to play their chosen piece.'

When my turn came, I began well enough but soon stumbled, and after a couple more clunky bars, could go no further. Everything I knew about playing, all the lessons Violet had taught me, went flying out of my head. My fingers were clumsy as sausages. None of the things I had learned or practised were available to me any more.

'I'm sorry, Miss Barnard. I don't know what's happened. I think I've forgotten how to play.'

'Oh dear – no, no, you haven't! Don't be silly. It's just I think we've rather put you on the spot. Perhaps you need a little time to gather yourself. Never mind and not to worry, Lola. Plenty of people – even the best of our musicians – come back after the holidays more than a little rusty and inconsistent. I've seen it again and again. We'll get you back in a rhythm in no time. Claudia, would you like to go instead please?'

Claudia was happy to go next and played a piece so perfectly and beautifully that it filled me with amazement for her and rage for myself.

'That was a bit cringe,' said Claudia after class when we got a chance to be introduced properly. 'Especially since everyone's saying you're some kind of musical prodigy.'

'I'm not, I'm really not,' I said as we ran from the music wing to be in time for tea.

I watched them all, but it was Allegra, day after day, who I watched the most. There was, I thought, an unfathomable effortlessness about her. The comfortable way she spread herself out when she sat on one of the library chairs and without looking, swung the arm of the lamp to shine the light on whatever she was reading. She was more sure of herself than anyone I'd ever met. That's what it was: a certainty in her that went all the way down into her bones and her gut and told her every day of her life that she would never have to fight or strive for her space in the world. Her space had always been there, waiting for her before she was born, and she occupied it now, the way a tree occupies its place in the forest, the way a queen occupies her place on a throne, the way the sun takes its place in the sky.

There was so much to get used to, but when I think of all the things that made Pearlbourne a stressful place, it was the packed schedule that was a major part of it – like a drum, it banged out its rhythm in the background of every day. The constant rush took a lot of getting used to. Breakfast was at seven. Early assembly was at eight. Class at eight thirty. Four periods before lunch, three periods afterwards. Extra-curricular activity was from four to six. Dinner from six to seven. Free time from seven to seven thirty. Prep and study hall for two hours after that. Supper at nine thirty. Bed and lights out at eleven.

Nothing but study and music and sport. No hanging around. No PlayStation, no Fifa, no throwing Frisbee out in the yard. Less time for boredom. More time for learning. A bell ringing after every well-planned chunk of time. Every moment designed to be full and round and rich, loaded with importance. Every activity planned to build and hone and develop the best of every Pearlbourne girl.

'I hear you totally screwed up in your consultation with Barney,' grinned Allegra on Friday when the morning bell rang.

'Who said that?' I asked.

'Claudia told me the whole thing. She and I are the same standard and have done all the same exams. She told me you haven't done any. Is it true?'

'Yes.'

'How long have you been at it?'

'Only a few months.'

'Hahahaha,' she laughed, and I hated the sound, all superior, all mockery. 'And to think I thought you were coming here to pose some stiff competition. Hahahaha.'

Turns out Allegra and Claudia had been having formal piano lessons since they were three.

At my next music lesson, I tried a lot harder and did my best to get to the end of the sonata. It was a bit better but you could see Miss Barnard was just being kind when she put her hands on my shoulders and said, 'Lola, thank you very much and yes, you're certainly worth working with.'

I'd been hoping she'd think I was brilliant, that I'd do some justice to the lie that I was related to Violet, but I'd learned a lot about standards of musicianship since I got here. Barney telling me I was worth a try should have been about as much as I could have expected.

She turned to a low table and began to scribble something in a book. 'If you work very hard indeed, you might, one day, be able to reach the standard of our Pearlbourne piano students. And so, from here on in, my advice to you is the same I give to everyone who comes here. Clichéd, perhaps, and overused, but it is honestly the truest I can give you. You get out what you put in.

'Simple as that, Lola. Listen to the accomplished girls we have nurtured in here. Let them be the lighthouses of your musical ambition.'

From then on, I promised I was going to throw my whole self into everything. I didn't want Allegra or Claudia to be my lighthouses. I wanted to be my own lighthouse. I didn't want to look up to them. I wanted to compete with them. If Violet ever came home, I wanted to be able to make her proud. Properly proud.

I wanted to be everyone at Pearlbourne. I wanted the uprightness and certainty of the teachers. I wanted the easy confidence of the students. I wanted the rich, colourful, eventful stories from their homes and all the things they took for granted, and I wanted the happy, unselfconscious way they joked and teased each other. Sometimes I found myself watching them for longer than was strictly polite, and I'd have to stop myself, and at night I worried if my gapes had been too blatant, and I'd remind myself how careful I had to be not to give myself away.

I became a magpie for every detail: the food they ate, the words they used, the way they walked. I grew deliberate about blinking the way they blinked and laughing the way they laughed and frowning the way they frowned, liking the things they liked and hating the things they hated. And all my concentration made a difference because every day I became less and less like Penny Nolan, Midgrey girl from The Flats, and more and more like Lola Nolan-Fitzsimons, Pearlbournian mystery girl of premium pedigree.

'Oh my god, you are so one of us,' Tilly Williams said one morning as I picked just the blueberries and the banana from the morning fruit salad. A warm feeling filled me up as I sat down at the long table for breakfast.

Quin and Jane and I had had a brilliant secret night-time chat in the third week, after Allegra had gone to sleep. Quin said how cool it was of me not to freak out about the trick she played. Jane reckoned Allegra really regretted doing it, not realising I was someone to be reckoned with, and I joined in the whispering and laughing in the darkness. It was great to be part of that conversation and it made me feel like the lies I told about myself were worth it.

After that, the weeks kept getting fuller and busier and I barely even had a second to think about home. When I did it made me shudder, the thought of the lonely darkness of my room, and the often-empty money jar, and Mam's cigarette smoke and the way it sometimes drifted under the gap of her bedroom door. And I'd hurl those memories right out of my head and wince under the covers at the very idea that Quin or Jane or Allegra would ever somehow know who I really was and where I really came from.

'Oh Lols,' said Quin one night, in her magnificent

227

velvety whisper. 'You know none of us was at all sure what to make of you when you first arrived.'

'How come?' I said, instantly wishing I hadn't asked.

'I don't know, we thought you seemed so wrong-footed, so starey.'

'Starey?'

'Yeah,' said Allegra, 'the way you stared at everything and everyone. It was weird.'

'I was new, guys, come on. New people have to take in the environment more than anyone else. It's called adjustment. It's called learning. And anyway, what's up with judging people for looking at things? That's harsh,' I said and they all laughed, a proper friendship kind of laugh that made me warm right down to the centre of my belly.

'Anyway, the point is, you don't do it any more, and we know you're cool and brilliant, and between us, we've decided you're one of the best things that's happened to Pearlbourne in a long time,' said Jane.

'Yeah, you see, when you first arrived, none of us really *got* you, you know, but now? Seriously, Lola, none of us can get over how well you're beginning to slot in, ' said Allegra.

'It honestly is as if you've always been here.' I could just make out Quin's shadow as she lay on her stomach on top of the covers.

'I can't even imagine Pearlbourne without you now,' said Jane, and the other two murmured in agreement.

I wondered when the three of them had got the

opportunity to talk about me in the early days and discuss in detail how they didn't know what to make of me. I didn't dwell on it, because they knew what to make of me now and everything was turning out OK.

All Pearlbournians had to stay for the first three weekends of term. It was a rule, to 'solidify the post-summer adjustment back to the rigours of the curriculum'. That's what the prospectus said. After that, people were free to go home on Fridays and come back on Sunday nights. But by then I'd decided there was no way I was going to. Even though I could afford it now, I didn't feel like wasting hundreds of euros on a driver, and would sometimes wake up in the night with my hair stuck to my face just thinking about the four hundred and thirty-nine euros I'd spent on the car to get here in the first place. Plus I worried that going home might break the spell.

All girls who didn't go home for the weekend after the third week were called 'stayovers'. I liked being called that. While most of the others lounged round the place watching movies or scrolling through their phones or reading books in the soft chairs in the library, I spent as much of my time as I could in the piano room. I practised pieces and phrases of pieces over and over again so that after my practice was over, I dreamed at night I was still playing. Even when I wasn't playing, or asleep, my fingers twitched and moved as if there were invisible piano keys everywhere.

Pierre Marmalody was our Home Ec teacher, a French chef with a booming voice who gave extra-curricular cooking classes to the stayovers on Saturdays from 8 a.m. till lunchtime and then we all got to sit down together and eat what we'd cooked.

On Sundays all stayovers normally went horse-riding. 'We can cover fifty miles cross-country and barely leave the Pearlbourne grounds,' said Allegra, who – according to Miss Allport – was by far 'our most accomplished rider'.

I wasn't going to tell anyone I'd only ever ridden a horse once and it hadn't even been a horse – it had been a donkey on a beach for like five minutes when I was six.

The others said horse-riding was what made the stayover weekends some of the best of their lives. They matched me with a mid-sized pony called Clayton, and I was clumsy and the others laughed at me but Clayton didn't seem to mind and happily galloped with me on his back through the Pearlbourne forests. He was such a brilliant, good-natured horse and his even temper and steady mood soothed me after the madness of the school week. I didn't much mind that we couldn't keep up with everyone else. I grew to enjoy the solitude and love that horse, and there was comfort in being able to tell him things about myself that he would not judge me for and secrets that no one else could ever learn.

On Sunday nights when the returners all piled in through the front entrance they smelled of the outside world, all metallic and chewing gum and traffic fumes, while we stayovers were still wrapped in the Pearlbourne blanket. Allegra was usually a stayover, and on the few weekends she did go home, she came back out of sorts and sulky and volatile and Jane and Quin and I gave her a wide berth because it would take until Monday morning assembly before she was herself again.

There were lots of other things about Pearlbourne that first were strange but gradually became normal. We were divided into groups called cantons and every morning we filed into the grand chamber assembly hall through one of six entrances – a door at each corner and two at the centre of each side wall, each a different colour. We lined up in alphabetical order by last name and when the bell rang, each row trailed into the huge room and took their places silently.

'Ahem,' Miss Lucas would begin.

The order of business was always dazzling. A list of achievements and personal bests attained during the previous week were read out with respect and celebration and polite applause. Rowing times, projects submitted, ground covered, progress made – it was all captured carefully by the teachers and recorded in the enormous 'Pearlbourne accomplishments' book.

I guess it made us all want to do our best. Getting into the accomplishments book mattered to everyone, even to the people who pretended not to care – maybe especially them. Success and failure had never been this visible at Midgrey and sometimes that fact filled me with determination and focus, but there were other times I had to admit I missed the lack of pressure a little bit. At Pearlbourne you knew where you stood in the league tables, and everyone else did too. Sometimes it was motivating. Other times it was depressing. Nothing's ever like you expect it's going to be.

I called Mam a few times but it was hard to talk. She'd say, 'How's it all going, lovey?' and I'd say, 'Grand, yeah, really good,' and she'd say, 'Well, that's great,' and I'd explain how I couldn't really go home for weekends because of all the work and she'd tell me she understood and that was pretty much all there was to say. I gave all my stayover parental permissions to the school using my fake email account, and that way the arrangements were kept under control.

Some weekends, a Special Saturday Party would be thrown at random. 'Weekends can be a lonely time for those who stay,' explained Miss Lucas when she announced, one Monday, the first midnight feast of the term, to a happy ripple of clapping and cheers.

Quin, Jane, Allegra and I had plenty of secret late-night snacking parties of our own, but formal Midnight Feast was held in the refectory. Candles were lit and they flickered and danced in a festive line along the table. The morning of the feast Pierre had taught us how to make loads of tiny canapés with piped soft cheese and little chunks of chutney topped with chives and baked crackers with one freshly-cooked prawn on each and crossed with an X of sweet chilli. And for after the savouries, we made our own petit fours with blobs of meringue, lightly toasted with miniature blow torches and sprinkled with lemon zest. 'Ladies,' he said. 'Not only are we preparing for tonight's wonderful feast, but you are also learning some of the essential skills of the hostess. Two birds, one stone!' he smiled, and everyone smiled back, looking delighted with themselves.

As I became more worried about breaking the Pearlbourne spell I got even less enthusiastic about leaving the grounds, not even when we were allowed to. On the fifth weekend, Allegra and Quin both stayed over and everyone got special leave tickets, which gave us permission to go into the nearby village of Clarenbridge.

'If everyone follows the rules then marvellous fun shall be had by all,' said Miss Lucas on the day the leave sheets were released. 'And as I hardly have to remind you, at all times, you are representing your school. Remember you are Pearlbournians. Extreme courtesy, clear diction, direct eye contact, upright deportment and all-round excellent conduct – they are the kinds of reports I want to hear. Thank you girls. Enjoy your weekend.'

Allegra fell in with me after Miss Lucas's speech. 'Hey Lola! Coming to Clarenbridge then?' she asked.

'No. I'm staying here. I've a few things to catch up on.'

'What a bore you are sometimes,' she said.

'How do you know? Shut up,' I answered and Allegra made a tut-tutting sound.

'Dear, dear, Lola Nolan-Fitzsimons or whatever you call yourself. "Shut up?" That's not very polite, is it? Remember you're a Pearlbournian now. Extreme courtesy, clear diction, direct eye contact. Look at me, Lola.'

But I refused. A chill rippled through me so strong I thought perhaps she could see it. I mumbled something about needing to get back to the dorm and sprinted away from her. Something about the way she'd talked to me had frightened me suddenly - something about the way she'd said, 'Or whatever you call yourself.'

And though I hoped it was just one of her stupid ways of talking, perhaps it was something else, and I didn't want to think about what that something might have been.

Everybody else was amazed I didn't want to go to Clarenbridge.

'Don't you long to escape from prison, even for a few hours?' asked Jane, genuinely mystified, her eyes rounder than ever.

'No, I'm getting extra lessons,' I explained, and maybe

234

Jane understood then. In any case, she stopped pestering me.

It was that weekend, when all the others were off buying sweets and comics in Clarenbridge, that Miss Barnard approached me in the library.

'Hello, Lola, how are you settling in?' she asked, looking deep into my eyes.

'Yeah, good,' I said.

'I must say, your playing is getting better and better. Every lesson you seem to have come on wonderfully. We're talking leaps. We're talking bounds.' And I was glad because I was working harder at this than at anything I'd ever worked at in my life and a lot of the time it felt like I was getting nowhere.

'I've noticed something else about you too,' she said and I could feel a prickle of nervousness creeping across me.

'What's that then?'

'Something has begun to happen when you play the piano. I've been thinking about it a great deal.'

'What do you mean?' I asked.

'I'm not sure,' she replied. 'You're at your most honest when you play, I think. These are the times when you're being truest to yourself. As if the rest of the time you are just pretending.'

Another flood of shock seeped through me. She was on

to me. Something swung open inside my body. I couldn't help blurting it out.

'I'm not who everyone thinks I am,' I began. I was about to tell her it all. How my family didn't have a villa on the Greek island of Spetses called The Captain's House, how I only knew about it because of a project I'd done in my old school, and how my old school was not a private boarding school in Sharjah, but a public day school called Midgrey near Blackrock. I could feel these truths dying to escape. I wanted to tell her that my mam was a cleaner, that I lived in The Flats. I felt ready suddenly for my big confession. Ready to admit and explain it all – prepared for the consequences.

CHAPTER 20

'Of course you're not who everyone thinks you are! Nobody here is, no need to look so worried about it,' said Miss Barnard. 'There isn't a girl in the place who doesn't have to put up some shield or wear some mask. I understand. It's a survival mechanism. Self-protection. You're no different from any of them. But it will be my job to find the truth in you. To seek it and to help you to declare yourself.'

I breathed out. OK, false alarm. So she wasn't on to me after all. She thought everyone else was just the same as me, and she thought I was just the same as everyone else.

After that, my drive to bring my standard up grew a bit obsessive, I suppose.

I began to stay late in the music room, going over things again and again. Focused on covering as much ground as I could to catch up with people who'd been getting lessons since they were three. One of those nights there was a knock on the piano room door. It was Daly.

'Gracious, what are you still doing here, Lola?'

'Practising,' I said.

'It's much too late. Your dorm head is probably doing the rounds now. Everyone else is probably already in bed.'

'I know, but I've so much to catch up on, Daly. You see, I haven't been learning piano for nearly as long as everyone else has.'

Daly sat on one of the chairs. He breathed in and breathed out and there was a little whistle in his nose, and he looked at me and I got the feeling he was going to share some wisdom, and then I'd go to bed with insights and understanding about myself and the school that would give me comfort and reassurance. But he just clapped his hands like he was shooing an animal out of a pen and said, 'Lola, stop being such an idiot would you and give up this lunacy. Get to your dorm, lively. This minute.'

I'd tried calling Violet many times, every evening at seven I always held out hope that I'd reach her, and then just as I was on the verge of giving up completely, finally, one night in October I got through. Her voice sounded terribly thin and very far away.

'Hello, dear darling girl,' Violet said. 'I've been longing to know how you're getting on.'

'Oh Violet, well it was tough at first, but I've stuck with it and things are great. I'm so thankful to you. This is an amazing opportunity and I'm grabbing it with both hands,' I said. Something cold shivered through me then, I wasn't sure why.

'Where are you, Violet?'

'I am on a long journey.'

'I wish you'd tell me where,' I said. 'I've been so worried.'

'I know, and I'm sorry but I simply cannot speak of it. And you mustn't worry. You need to focus on where you are right now. You've no time to be worrying about old ladies. Now run along back to the schedule, and say hello to the maths garden for me, if it's still there. And look for my name on the wall of girls!'

And her voice (or was it the line?) seemed to be fading and I told her again what a brilliant gift she had given me and she kept saying how she couldn't be happier with the way everything sounded like it was turning out. And then the phone connection fizzled and died completely.

I got better and better at assuming my identity as a Pearlbourne girl. But there were traps everywhere, and sometimes they would creep up on me just when I had begun to feel I'd cracked it. One night we had a special third-year dinner, where the food was served to us by the first years and we had three courses all made by them with Pierre

239

Marmalody as meal supervisor. 'Bon appétit,' said a girl I'd never met who plonked herself beside me.

'Lola Nolan-Fitzsimons,' I replied.

'No, bon appétit,' said the girl a bit louder.

And I said, 'Lola Nolan-Fitzsimons,' even louder and the girl whose name I thought was Bon, looked at me funny and I noticed Allegra smiling on the other side.

'That's not her name, you ninny!' she shouted. 'Cecile is her name, and she's telling you to have a nice meal in French.'

'I knew that,' I replied and Cecile laughed really loud and Allegra quietly looked at me with her head at an angle.

Moments later I told Allegra the soup was cold and she said, 'Lols, it's gazpacho. It's *supposed* to be cold.'

But I continued to make huge leaps forward in my standard of piano playing. Miss Barnard said it was a phenomenon that sometimes happened to very motivated students. It all came from the ingredients I'd been bringing to my practice. She said my focus was incredible, and that I was learning to loosen up and relax into the playing; and she'd noticed how I always prepared so carefully, including the things that lots of people don't bother with – like how I warmed up my fingers and how I practised a lot of different elements at every session and how I would repeat and repeat until I'd smoothed out all the edges of a piece, and how I was practically religious about doing my scales and arpeggios, and how I never scrimped on the boring bits of the work like the technical aspects and sight-reading. I researched each new piece thoroughly, learning about the composer and what was going on for them at the time they wrote it, and I separated the parts for each hand before bringing the whole thing together, and I'd learned not to try something fast until I'd mastered playing it slow, and I concentrated on the musical and the precision and the passion all together.

She said it was extraordinary. She started talking about me to the other students, saying things like, 'This is what's possible when someone tries their very best,' and I knew then that I was catching up and the gap between me and Claudia and Allegra was closing.

Perhaps it was a coincidence but this was also the time that Allegra's mean side started coming out again. Back at our dorm after the third-year dinner, Allegra started with the quizzing.

'Who are you, Lola, I mean who are you really?' she hissed at me in the dark.

'I've no idea what you mean. I'm Lola Nolan-Fitzsimons.'

'Yes, but who is Lola Nolan-Fitzsimons? I've never met anyone like you before. I'd really like to know more about you.'

'I'm not unusual,' I said as casually as I could.

'Yes you are!' said Allegra. 'Very. I've never met anyone who doesn't know what bon appétit means, and doesn't know gazpacho is served chilled, and doesn't know the basics about riding a pony. And you called Connie Minton-Holmes a 'mam'. Like, what's that all about? I mean, where have you been all your life? I'm beginning to wonder if you are who you say you are at all.'

'Oh god,' I exhaled. 'All right. You're on to me. I suppose I'd better explain.'

I could hear Jane and Quin holding their breath too, listening.

'Firstly, as a child, I was very allergic to horses, and it's a condition I've only recently got over. It's why I'm a little clumsy on the back of a horse. Secondly, of course I know what bon appétit means. I told you, I was only joking with Cecile. A stupid joke maybe, but you know, I'm still trying to break the ice with a lot of people. Mam, mama, mum, whatever, give me a break, and for your info, not everyone has eaten gazpacho. I'm actually surprised at you, Allegra, being so ethnocentric.'

'Yeah,' said Quin, 'stop being so ethnocentric.'

'What does that mean?' asked Allegra.

'See? There are things you don't know either!' said Jane and I loved the way she always defended me.

I crossed my arms over my chest and said, 'I rest my case,' making sure to keep quite a posh, superior tone in my voice.

'Ethnocentric,' I explained, 'is assuming everyone has experienced all the things you've experienced in life. And it's wrong to make those assumptions.'

*

Another time, Allegra fell in with me as we filed out of the ref one night after milk and singing. 'What was it like in Sharjah?' she whispered. 'What did you eat? What did you do after study? Same as here? Or different?'

I was put with Selena Perry and Georgia Price for a history project. We stayed up until three o'clock in the morning animating our slide transitions, editing in a backing track. The presentation wiped the floor with everyone else. I made sure it was going to. Selena and Georgia hugged me and together the three of us did the Pearlbourne squeal.

'This is the first A1 I've ever got,' Selena cheered, and everyone knew it was because of me.

I never really got the hang of tennis and stopped trying after a while, and rowing was another challenge. It chilled me the way all these things seemed to come so naturally to everyone else. I never got the total hang of horse-riding either but I did get better and was very attached to my friendly Clayton, who whinnied every time I visited him in his stables and he didn't ever seem to care what little clue I had about the proper way to ride a horse.

Each morning I got up ninety minutes before everyone else and crept down to the music wing to get some extra practice in, then flew up to the ref for breakfast before anyone knew. I was going to keep practising and I would not stop until Claudia and Allegra were spellbound by me, and everyone else was too.

Allegra kept going on about how she'd never been to Greece. That's how she started, and then when Halloween was coming up – called The Hallow Break by Pearlbourne girls – she began what can only be described as a campaign.

'Seriously, I mean it – what about Lola's fam's place in Greece?' she said casually during one of our late-night chats.

'Oh my god, yes!' Quin practically catapulted out of bed. 'We're so sick of Tuscany, and we've been to Provence hundreds of times, and your place is too far for just a long weekend, Allegra, but none of us has ever been to Greece. So how about it, Lola Nola? It's rather the tradition for The Hallow Break.'

'What is?' I asked, mystified.

'Dorm sisters take The Hallow Break together. We've all taken turns about whose house to go to, but Greece! How exotic and different from dull old Tuscany and the overcrowded Riviera. And no one wants to go to Allegra's parents' place any more. You're barely over the jetlag when we have to go home again. Oh, come on, do, do, Lola. We love the idea of Greece. Please let's go.'

'Yes,' said Allegra, dabbing her face with moisturiser from a golden jar.

'Greece for half term!'

'Spetses! Spetses! Spetses!' chanted Quin and Allegra.

'Stop it everyone,' said Jane, putting the brakes on. 'Bloody hell, the two of you scrabbling and bleating. Give her some space, stop pestering her.'

'We're not pestering!' they said.

'Yes you are. It's just so pushy. She's barely here a few weeks and you two are already trying to blag a hol in her gaff. How previous of you both. Leave her alone. She might have decided she cannot stand us, mightn't you, Lola? It's likely she'll be so sick of us all by the time Hallow Break is here she won't want to spend another single second with any of us.'

'In your case, not likely,' I said to Jane, and I could tell she was delighted.

As the time wound on, I became more committed to my lies. I even thought I might pull off hosting an actual holiday in Greece, in the exact house I pretended belonged to my family. It was available for rent, and well, I had the means now, as Violet would have put it. I spent a week or more feeling fairly sure I could organise it. I could go to Spetses ahead of time to smooth the way and make it seem as if the house really did belong to the family I had invented.

But in the end, I slapped myself in the face, literally, one night when I'd woken up and realised this would be crazy – an endeavour of Icarian proportions. Attempting it would be my downfall. That night, there in the dark with my heart clattering again inside my chest, I decided it would be better and wiser to do what I ended up doing.

'Guys, look, I'm sorry to disappoint you, but our place in Greece is a no-go. Mummy and Daddy are lending it to old friends of ours during the half term break, and there simply would not be enough room for us all.'

I told Allegra I was planning to stay in Pearlbourne for The Hallow Break.

'How awfully odd,' was all she said and in the dark I imagined her eyes doing their Allegra flicker full of flint and steel as a little moment of truth seemed to hover between us.

'You do know you'll be the only girl here,' said Quin. 'You'll be like a ghost, haunting the dorms and the corridors.' And again, I felt like a stranger. But it was just a moment and it passed.

Having Pearlbourne to myself was a brilliant, wonderful thing. I had time to wander through the halls and corridors and stop and look at things properly, not rushing by in a blur. I went to the main hallway and studied the wall of girls, which had the names of every single student who'd graduated from Pearlbourne since the year of its foundation in 1789. I found Violet's name – she left the school in 1958. I could not find her sister.

Miss Barnard stayed with me for the whole week – possibly the greatest coup of my life. And Daly almost always seemed to be on hand to see if we had everything we needed. On the first night of the hols, the three of us had cocoa together in the ref.

I would be in the piano room, Miss Barnard knew, if ever she was looking for me. Practising, practising. Perhaps it became a kind of madness, not that Miss Barnard ever saw anything wrong with it. 'There are many reasons I am glad you have come here. I see a hunger in you,' she said. 'I see a longing for development and for improvement, and you know, you are the kind of student I have always wanted in my music studio. I have several good students, but some of them are plateauing. None of them push themselves like you have done. And you really are catching up, just as you said you would – nipping at the heels of the others.' She waited till the end of the week to tell me that I was in with a real chance of getting a slot at the Winter open concert.

During Hallow Break Pierre got wind of how I was always in the piano room and argued it was unhealthy, so partly to keep him happy and partly in honour of Violet, I made a cherry pie in the kitchen. And I texted Violet a photo of it, and a second photo of a slice of it with a big blob of whipped cream on top, but Violet did not text back and I worried a bit. But if I'm really honest, I didn't think that much about her, or about Matt or Kitty or Mam or Vlad or Breda or Tony or anyone from The Flats. It was like

Pearlbourne rubbed out your memory and made you alert for the ringing of a bell, even at the weekend when the bells did not ring. Miss Barnard and I rowed on the Pearlbourne lake and it felt like my own personal holiday, and I never regretted it, and in a way I never will, not even when other girls came back with ski-goggle tans and Italian chocolates and a hundred stories of overseas colour and delight.

Midgrey and The Flats seemed to get more and more remote. I did text Kitty and Matt sometimes but it got harder and harder to know what to say to them. And I'd still call Mam but our conversations stayed short and I didn't like it when she said she missed me, and I didn't like how ashamed I felt for being at Pearlbourne while she was still in The Flats, cleaning other people's toilets and not having enough money for even the smallest of treats. I was haunted sometimes by the echoes of my old life. At strange times, funny memories like Mr Galloway's discouragements would float into my mind again – all those things he used to say about pride coming before a fall, about how it doesn't do to get above yourself, how people shouldn't always fly as high as they might want to.

Not long after Hallow Break, I caught up with Claudia and Allegra when we were on our way to Italian with Senorina Vignano. 'Guys, I just wanted to say thank you!'

'For what?' said Allegra.

'For helping me up my musical game. Miss Barnard says I might be in contention for the Winter concert performance. Wouldn't it be brill, the three of us playing on stage together?'

'Fab,' Claudia replied, and with her eyes she did the Pearlbourne blink – slow, slightly indifferent.

'Amazing,' Allegra said, doing the same.

The first concert of the year was scheduled for the beginning of December, and by then it had started to get dark at five. The fires were all lit and roaring, and Pearlbourne Academy looked brilliant with the windows bright and all the music rising from it. Parents were invited, and by six, the sound of big wheels crunching up the drive made my nerves even more fluttery, and I kept thinking about how hard I'd worked to get here and telling myself to take deep breaths and not to screw it up.

The concert was in the hall with the glass roof so we could look up at the stars. There were lots of performances lined up, but Allegra, Claudia and I were doing the opening and the closing, and everyone knew we were the stars of the show. A full moon shone down like a polished coin on all three of us as we took our seats and played for the audience of teachers and parents and Pearlbourne girls who stood when we finished and shouted, 'BRAVA!

BRAVA!' over and over again and Miss Barnard placed a gigantic bouquet of roses each into our arms.

I should have invited my mam, I thought. I probably should have invited Matt and Kitty and Breda and Tony and even Vlad. They'd have been amazed to see me doing what I did. The only person I invited was Violet but I couldn't bear to think about any of the possible reasons why she wasn't replying and why she didn't come so I put those thoughts out of my head, and stayed focused on my goals.

There was another high point. It came just after the concert when the votes for spring prefect were cast. The process was simple – just a wooden box in the third-year common room. On a ballot paper, the girls had to put the name of the person they wanted and fold it up and post it in.

A special count was organised in the ref with cocoa and cherry pie which reminded me of Violet again.

I'd never expected to be voted in. Everyone thought it would be Allegra or Caroline Jordan or maybe Quin or Claudia. Miss Lucas presided over the count and the numbers were triple-checked and on each check, the name at the top of the poll, by a long distance, was mine.

They put me up on their shoulders and carried me around the school and then we ran out on to the lawn and everybody cheered and clapped and I didn't think it would be possible to feel so much pride and so much loyalty to a place.

In a way it was the blink of an eye. In a way it was a whole lifetime. In a way it was just a dream.

Then there was a special ceremony where I was given a Pearlbourne badge – still have it – and from then on everyone referred to me as 'Lola Nolan-Fitzsimons: prefect-designate' and for the rest of the term Genie Calorglin was to teach me all the responsibilities and ways of the prefect role.

From then on, because of me, ours was the dorm everyone gathered in for midnight chats.

I hardly saw Millie Minton-Holmes the whole rest of the semester. She was in fifth year, and as she'd told me herself, there wasn't much chance to hang out with us, though she would smile sometimes and wave at me from her horse when we were out at cross-country, or she might hold her mug of cocoa up from the other side of the ref if we caught each other's eye, and it felt good to have a senior girl so firmly in my corner. She may have been the saving of me, I often thought.

It was Millie though who knocked me off Clayton one Sunday at cross-country. I'm still not sure what happened exactly, only that she came galloping straight for me. Later she claimed her horse had got excited and she hadn't been able to control him. Miss Fatharay had seen the collision in motion and before it happened had roared from the quadrangle:

'MINTON-HOLMES! HALT YOUR HORSE.'

But Millie did not halt her horse and they crashed into us. The sturdy and unflappable Clayton did his best and managed to stay upright, but I fell off him completely. A lot of the rest is a blank. Loud voices, stretchers, some talk between Miss Lucas and Mrs Halloran that my parents should be contacted, which jolted me out of my semi-consciousness.

'DO NOT CONTACT MY PARENTS!' was all I'd been able to say, and there was the noise of relieved laughter and the claim there couldn't be much wrong with me if I'd had the wherewithal to shout instructions in this way. They thought it was just me being brave and stoic, exercising the Pearlbournian trait of not wanting to cause a fuss.

Nurse Byrne in sick bay, who'd only ever given me lessons in hygiene and nutrition, seemed positively elated suddenly to have a meaningful project. She insisted on testing my eyesight by shining a sharp-lit torch into my pupils and gauged my balance by making me walk in a straight line in the infirmary. After I'd passed those tests, she sat me down.

'How many fingers am I holding up?' she asked.

'I'm fine, Nurse, honestly.'

'How many?' she said more sternly.

'Two.'

'OK, good. Now is there any bruising? Let me look.'

She began pressing different parts of my skull.

'I'm really fine. There is nothing wrong with me. Nothing hurts at all.'

'Right well, one thing's for sure – that's the end of activities for you this evening, madam. I'll be bringing you straight to bed. And once there, you mustn't move until the morning and we'll check again and see how you are then. Do I make myself clear?'

I slept and woke and slept and woke, dreaming of Kitty and Matt and thinking about Violet and Matt's grandparents and my mam. By then they might as well have been in another universe, so dense was the space between my old life and this one.

Under other circumstances, I'd have sat up as soon as I heard my dorm sisters come in. But Nurse Byrne had told me to lie still, even if I was awake, and besides, Quin, Allegra and Jane were deep in the thick of an intense conversation. It quickly became obvious they were talking about me.

'Millie told me the first time she met her was when she came to her house with a ladder and a bucket, offering to clean their windows,' said Quin,

'How awfully extraordinary,' said Allegra.

'I thought they met in Dubai or Greece or somewhere,' said Jane.

'Nope. Millie doesn't really know anything about her,' said Quin.

'No one's ever met her parents. No one has ever been to her house, been out to dinner with her family, nothing,'

Allegra went on. 'There is something weird about that, don't you think?'

'Come on, stop being so ridic,' said Jane. 'There are loads of people whose parents no one's met. That's not one bit unusual.'

'I mean, we all know she's a superstar and everything and we all love her and how well she's got stuck in here, but there is still something. I can't put my finger on it.' From the stillness of my bed I could hear that tone in Allegra's voice. She was on one of her rolls. 'I mean, she wasn't even that good at piano when she first came here. It's as if she's been possessed by demons all that practising she does. And now she's lined herself up to barge in on myself and Claudia's performances for evermore.'

'But we thought you loved her joining in,' said Quin.

'I know what must have happened.' Allegra was seething now, barely listening to the others. 'She must have cornered Barney during Hallow Break when she had her to herself. Obviously she put pressure on Barney. And you know, Claudia and I are almost thinking of giving up piano and moving on to viola.

'And another thing, don't you think it's really weird the way she doesn't talk about her family? How deliberately foggy she is about her past?'

'Some people don't like talking about their home lives,' Jane tried, but Allegra was really ranting now.

'And one day I picked up her diary and a picture fell out

of it – a picture of two very rough-looking children. They were standing outside what can only be described as a tenement with a terrible beat-up car in the background. And exactly who keeps a picture of those kinds of people in their diaries? Why on earth would she have a photograph of them at all? And do you remember how often she didn't answer when we called her by her name, near the beginning of term? There was actually a while when I thought maybe she needed to have her hearing tested but now I think it's something else.'

'Steady on, Allegra,' said Jane, but Allegra did not steady on. She just kept going.

'You know something? I think there's quite a good chance that Lola Nolan-Fitzsimons is not her real name. I have a sense there were times when she forgot that's what she'd decided to call herself. Don't you understand? I think Lola may be some kind of spy, some kind of fraud. Here for evil reasons none of us knows about. We must tread very carefully. We may all be in terrible danger.'

I lay still and flat, trying barely to breathe.

Jane was taking over now and I loved her for it.

'Allegra, you simply must stop this nonsense without delay. You are being perfectly horrendous. Of course she's not a spy or a fraud. Since when does someone have to tell you things she doesn't want to talk about? You're just annoyed that you don't know everything about her. But whether you like it or not, Allegra, she has a right to her

255

privacy. Everyone does. And OK, we didn't get to go to Greece, but it's not a reason to be suspicious of her. In any case, she's incoming prefect now.'

'There's another thing. Incoming prefect? She's barely here a wet week and she's been voted in as prefect? Wait till you see, I bet she'll back out of the prefect-designate party too.'

There was a rustle and a whisper.

'Shh,' said Quin, 'look. She's here, in the bed,' and the three of them went very quiet. 'Byrney must have brought her back from infirmary.'

'We could have woken her. She could have heard us,' whispered Jane.

'No way, she got a terrible bang. She's conked out, sleeping it off, she can't hear a thing,' whispered Allegra. I kept a deliberate rhythm in my breath and my eyes closed as they all satisfied themselves no damage had been done.

'Can I just say one more thing,' said Allegra. I could hear them pulling off their clothes and sliding into their silken PJs. 'I know someone whose cousin goes to Sharjah International, and I Insta'd them the other day and guess what?'

My blood stopped flowing in my veins.

'They don't ever remember a Lola Nolan-Fitzsimons going there. Not last year. Not the year before. Not ever.'

'Oh Allegra, now this really is just so ridiculous,' said Jane. 'Why would Lola lie? Stop being such a stalker.'

The bell rang for supper, and the three of them banged around the place and flew back out through the door.

The silence they left behind was full of a kind of static. I rolled over and rubbed my eyes and there were those sparks again at the edges of my sight. Little bursts of fear seemed to explode inside me. I texted Genie Calorglin.

'Hey Genie. What's the prefect-designate party?'

'OMG,' she replied. 'How could I have forgotten to tell you? It's a thing all incoming prefects do. They host a between-term party in their house, wherever it is, and everyone in the year comes, and it's a way of celebrating you and it's one of the best things about being prefect – you get to see everyone in your place when you're home for the hols. Normally early Jan, just before we go back.'

I remembered then that Violet had told me about Lavender House being host to many such parties long ago. How Violet had been prefect several times. How she'd conducted herself with the grace of the victor, how all the girls arrived at the front, dressed in silk and taffeta, and gathered together in Violet's own golden spaces, playing piano and singing songs – the Pearlbourne spirit glowing in the air.

I thought about Matt and Kitty then, with a sudden unexpected lurch in my stomach like I might get sick. Our texts to each other had almost dried up. I can't remember if it was me who stopped texting them, or them who stopped texting me. I thought about sending them an apology. I thought about asking for their help. I wondered what Christmas back home in The Flats was going to be like but in the end I didn't text them at all. I texted Violet.

'Violet are you there?'

'Violet where are you?'

My dorm sisters were still talking about me when they got back from supper. 'It's fairly typical of trust-fund kids to need to change their names,' Jane was explaining. 'Maybe she used a different name over there. Maybe the Sharjah boarders keep studentship confidential to prying external eyes. Anyway, Lola doesn't have to prove anything to anyone. She's one of us. We shouldn't second-guess her and we should take her as she comes and leave it at that.'

It was comforting to hear the faith Jane had in me and because of it, my blood stopped rushing through my veins. I was going to use Violet's house. I had the key. There would be lots to do. I'd make it the best Pearlbourne party ever and Allegra would stop doubting me, and everything was going to be all right.

CHAPTER 21

Pearlbourne looks like a fable at Christmastime. They put a huge tree in the assembly hall and thousands of tiny lights in the trees on the lawn and a giant wreath at the front entrance, and everywhere smells of cinnamon and mandarin oranges and cloves, and they make this fruit cake and a thing called brandy butter which I'm not even sure is legal if you're under eighteen but it's a Pearlbourne tradition and nobody has ever questioned it.

Towards the end of term, the days zoomed by and the talk was suddenly about plans for the holidays: skiing on mountains in France; sunshine breaks in Sydney or Florida, and big gatherings in brilliant places where there would be no bells ringing and no study halls and no projects and no rules and the truth is that being in boarding school is mainly quite hard work and by Christmas everyone needed a break.

Everyone apart from me. I didn't even want to think

about going back to The Flats. I hadn't talked to anyone there for ages. Before I came here, I'd thought it would be a simple thing. Going from The Flats to Pearlbourne and back again. But it didn't feel simple any more.

I remember how I clung to those last days in the school, often waking early in the winter dark.

We were allowed to light a real fire in the small grate of our dorm and we talked till very late, way after lights out. And when the rest of them were asleep I would sometimes stare at the ceiling in the dark, trying to make out the shapes – its elaborate plaster with angels and fruit and musical instruments, and sometimes tears would fall out of my eyes and drip down into my ears. I didn't want to leave. I wondered whether anyone had ever stayed over the Christmas break – and if it wasn't for having a party to organise, I might even have looked into it. As it was, I made up invitations and everyone said that wherever they were going to be at Christmas, they would definitely come back for my party. Some were going to fly in especially. January third. A great last blast before the new term. That's what everyone said it was going to be.

Mam looked different when I got home. I think she'd got her hair done. There were candles lit on the counter. The sight of the money jar made something deep and shameful stir inside me.

'Oh Penny, look at you, I'd hardly know you!' she said, all excited.

'I've got cheese on toast ready for you and your favourite orange juice and oh love, I've missed you so much. I barely even recognise your voice! Thought you'd never come.'

I told her I didn't really eat cheese on toast any more.

'What?' said Mam. 'But cheese on toast is the best. Your favourite.'

'I know, but right now I'd just like to have a piece of fruit, please, and maybe a yoghurt, and are there any rice cakes in the house?'

She looked at me and said, 'Rice cakes?' and I smiled and apologised, remembering where I was and that in the history of this galley kitchen, there'd never been a single rice cake here.

Mam wanted to know all about Pearlbourne, but Pearlbourne felt like another planet now too and talking about it would be like speaking in a different language and there was nothing about any of it I could explain.

'Mam, it's great,' was all I said, shoving my luggage into my room and sitting up on my old stool. 'It's a great school. I'm getting on brilliant.'

I drank the tea she made, and nibbled on a Ritz cracker, but I was suddenly very tired and told Mam I'd prefer to go to bed and would she mind leaving all the talk to the morning.

'Have you seen Kitty or Matt yet?'

I told her I hadn't.

261

'You'd better let them know you're home. They've spent the whole time asking about you. I ran out of things to tell them.'

'I don't think they're too thrilled with me. I've been really bad about checking in with anyone,' I said.

The flat smelled better than I remembered, but the kitchen window was still painted shut and there were still the bangs and murmurs of other people's lives from behind the partition walls. I wandered back into my old room. No sign of the damp patches but still it felt like all my joy was gone. The thin bed. My makeshift desk, all the books I'd left behind. I used to think it was a super collection, but it just looked flimsy and ragged and unimportant compared to the magnificent books I could read any day of the week in the Pearlbourne library.

I texted Kitty and Matt.

Two minutes later Matt was at the door, grinning like I'd never been gone, and I thought I'd be glad to see him but I felt sad, like there was some invisible distance between us that I couldn't do anything about.

'Where's Kitty?'

'Here she is now.'

Kitty looked wrecked but maybe she just looked the way I used to look.

'Kitty, hello.'

'Hello,' she replied. 'You look . . . I mean wow . . . you look really great. I've missed you.'

I told her I'd missed her too.

'You look really different,' Matt said but he didn't say if he meant different good or different bad and I didn't ask.

'You look just the same,' I said.

I was glad when we left for my Aunt Allie's a few days before Christmas. The Pearlbourne party was still on for January third. When you have the kind of money I was getting used to having, you can get a lot done by phone. You don't even have to be there. I sent Millie Minton-Holmes's gardening team round to bring Violet's front garden under control.

'Focus on the entrance,' I told them.

When you're a person of means planning a party like I was, these things are not so hard – it's just a matter of making a decision and then sticking with it.

Christmas at Auntie Allie's was fine. There were fewer questions and loads of kids running around and less of a focus on me, and I could disappear without anyone noticing and I kept it to myself, the mad secret fever I was in to get Lavender House ready.

We got home on December twenty-ninth. I sneaked next door, wrapped my hands around the freezing cold bars of

Violet's front gates and gasped. Millie Minton-Holmes's gardener had done a perfect job. Everything had been tidied up: the marble bench, the lily pond, the white statue, the flowers and even the front door, glossy with fresh paint, and the dolphin in the middle glistening from a recent polish, like it was about to leap into the gleaming pond itself.

Strictly speaking, it was a terrible thing I was doing here. I had no permission from Violet. I was taking over her house under false pretences and gaining access to it without her knowledge, and if I'd allowed myself to think about all this, perhaps I would have lost my nerve. So I did what I had become skilled at: I blotted it out. 'I am Lola Nolan-Fitzsimons,' I kept telling myself. 'I'm a talented, important person and this is my home and I will host the best party my fellow Pearlbournians have ever been at. I shall succeed, and I shall perform and I shall entertain.'

Keeping busy. That was the important thing. There was no time for sitting around The Flats. I didn't belong there any more, mulling over my old life, worrying about whether I was doing the right thing or not. 'I am committed and I have to follow through, because that is who I am,' I told myself. There was still a lot to do as January third approached. I bought tons of garden lights and I ordered the delivery of a massive Christmas tree.

'What are you up to?' Mam said one evening as my phone kept buzzing, skittering around on the kitchen counter every five minutes or so.

'Oh, me? I'm involved in a thing for Violet Fitzsimons next door.'

'I thought she'd gone away.'

'Yep, she's back for a few days. Hosting a party.'

'Oh, right,' said Mam and she didn't ask me any more about it.

Jane and Quin phoned every day. Whenever we talked about the party, they did the Pearlbourne squeal.

And in the days leading up to the party, I spent most of the time ignoring Matt and Kitty's texts because I was busy in Lavender House dusting and sweeping and cleaning and pulling the sheets off the furniture and off the piano and remembering the days I had sat at the piano and played so dreadfully for Violet.

I bought a green silk dress in Brown Thomas and took a photo in the changing room to send to Quin and Jane and Allegra.

'Stunning!' 'Fabulous!' 'OMG it's PERFECT' came their answers, beep beep beep all in a row.

They sent me photos of what they were going to wear, and I got confirmations from almost all the teachers, including Miss Lucas – which was a really big deal – and Miss Lucas emailed me to say that this was going to be an historic occasion, considering how Lavender House was such a special part of Pearlbourne's history already and how my great-aunt must be so proud of me. I tried to put thoughts of Violet out of my head. It was going to be one of the best Pearlbourne parties in the history of the school.

I ordered the catering from Butler's Pantry on recommendation from Millie, and talked them through the menu and made sure there were going to be plenty of canapés and petit fours and everything was going to be as glorious as I could make it: sushi too, and elderflower sparkling water, and homemade ice cream and little bundles of chocolate in pouches tied with gold string for going home. I'd planned the music for the whole night. I asked Claudia to bring her viola and Cecile to bring her harp if she could manage it, and between us by email we agreed the running order. And I bought a load of new candles to put in Violet's many shining silver candlesticks and I put burning wood in Violet's oven in the huge kitchen and I cranked up the heating and soon the place no longer had the empty feeling and was as warm and festive as any lived-in mansion could be.

I tried calling Violet again, partly out of guilt because of all the presumptions I'd made and partly out of hope of hearing her voice. But in a way I was glad she didn't answer. I'm not sure what I would have said.

I told Mam I'd be staying over next door and she said, 'OK lovey, if that's what you want.'

I left the flat carrying my new dress over one arm, and a bag full of make-up and a last few things for the party in the other. I was halfway down the stairs when I heard the shout.

'Penny!'

He was standing at the bottom, staring at me with a strange wobbly look on his face. 'Penny. You off?'

'Oh Matt, look I know we need a proper catch-up. I really want one. It's just been a bit hectic. Like I've hardly had a moment since I got back, and now I'm doing this thing next door for Violet.'

'What thing?' he asked.

'A kind of event I'm sort of helping to host at Lavender House.'

'That's good of you, Penny. Make sure you let us know if you need any help.'

'Ah no, I'm grand thanks,' I said. 'But maybe I'll see you and Kitty tomorrow? I won't be so busy after tonight and I'm still around for a couple more days.'

'Yeah,' he said. 'Maybe. I might be free.' And I didn't know what else to say and besides time was getting close and I needed to go.

'I called you, Penny,' he said as I made my way towards the exit.

'What?'

'I called you a thousand times.' He walked off back up the stairs, with his hands in his pockets and his shoulders hunched and there just wasn't time. Right then I had to stay focused. This was the most important evening in my career as a Pearlbournian and it was vital everything went perfectly. If anyone at Pearlbourne had

267

doubts about me, tonight would banish those doubts forever.

I opened the gates and turned on the garden lights and the lily pond shimmered in the crisp of the January evening and I turned on the chandelier in the hall and I let the caterers in with their big white boxes full of food.

'Go on in through to the kitchen, please,' I said, as if I really did own the place.

There were more beautiful rooms upstairs in Violet's house. I silenced the voices inside me that said I should not trespass and found her big bedroom and pulled the dust covers off her bed and her armchairs and I had a bath in her bathroom and dried myself with fluffy white towels from the cupboard and put my make-up on in her mirror and slipped my silk green dress over my head and pushed my toes into my emerald-green shoes and I walked down the glittering Lavender House stairway and checked the piano room for the tenth time, and wandered around making sure everything was perfect. And it was.

I'd done it, I told myself. There was still half an hour to go. I could relax, take a moment to get my head in the game before everyone started to arrive. I sat on one of Violet's tapestry chairs and remembered the day I rescued Bluebell and wondered where she was now. I thought about meeting Violet here and how that first day she'd held a knife to protect herself from the outside world – and how well we got to know each other after that and how she was now in some distant place where I could not reach her. And I saw again her old elegant beauty, and her fingers, and her almond-shaped nails, and I heard her music playing.

A flash on my phone jolted me back into the moment.

'Penny. It's me Kitty. I'm here. Outside the door. Let me in.'

I opened the door. Kitty stood firmly with her feet apart, her hands on her hips. 'I need to talk to you,' she said.

'Kitty, listen, now is not the time.'

'When is the time then?' she said, not budging.

'Tomorrow. I already said it to Matt, I met him on the stairs. Did he not say? You and me and him are meeting up tomorrow.'

'Yeah, I spoke to him. He told me not to come here, but I don't know if I can trust you to be around tomorrow. I wanted to see you tonight, to give you a chance.'

'What do you mean by that?'

'A chance to prove you haven't totally turned your back on us. Like, Penny, we're your friends. Your oldest friends, and it feels like we've lost you.'

I glanced at the phone in my hand, because time was flying and Kitty really needed to be gone before any of my guests arrived.

'You haven't lost me,' I said weakly.

'Then let us come tonight? Me and Matt? We could all hang out together. It would be fun.'

'NO!' I said, louder than I'd wanted to, and Kitty blinked. 'Stop it, Kitty. You can't just barge in on this. You're not invited, and neither is Matt, right? This is not about you. I've things to think about and things to do and to be honest, it's unfair of you to turn up like this and make these demands on me.'

In the light of Lavender House's grand entrance, Kitty's face was very white. 'I'm sorry,' she said. 'I didn't mean to be demanding. I'll go and leave you to it.'

'Thank you,' I said.

'Do you know how important you are to me?' she said. 'Me and Matt.'

'Please stop this,' I said.

'No seriously. You used to rescue me every day. You've heard the way my mam shouts at me in the night. You know how I have no power to do anything about it. But you were always there, every day, and then one day you just left. I never even get to see you now, not even when you're home. You barely bother to answer my texts.'

'Kitty, look, I keep telling you we can talk about all this tomorrow. Just not now.'

'OK,' she said. 'Sorry for intruding on your time. You're still important to me, Penny, even if I'm not that important to you.'

And she turned and her steps were slow on the granite and I watched as she walked down the garden, past the marble bench and through the gates.

*

The beginning of that night is like a fairy-tale dream to me still. My fellow Pearlbournians swooshing up to the front gates in sleek cars and hopping out and clip-clopping along the freshly-weeded stone path, and me standing in the doorway, welcoming them in.

Everyone loved the house and the food and we all played music together and Miss Lucas gave a speech and told us that of each of the prefect-designate parties she'd been at through the years, this topped them all, and there were cheers and toasts and more music and laughter and celebration. I felt as if I was drunk from the happiness of having cemented my place at Pearlbourne, drunk with thoughts of all the brilliant terms that were still to come. And my three dorm sisters were sparkling with pride. Even Allegra's smile seemed broad and clear and true.

'You know a few of us thought you were making all this up!' Claudia said with her arm around me. 'I'm ashamed to say it now, but we thought you were a fake. We're so sorry for doubting you. I'm so glad we are friends. So glad you've invited us to this brilliant home. So glad you're one of us.'

Everyone gathered in the piano room, and I delivered it, the best version of Sonata number eight I'd ever done. There was total hush and amazement followed by great applause and I could see tears in Miss Barnard's eyes. This was it, it really was. All the practice, all the pretence, all the persistence – all my dreams coming true. I was too dazzled to see that there were other things happening.

I hadn't noticed that Allegra had taken up a prominent spot in the middle of the room. She was tinkling a silver spoon on her glass and then she shouted, 'LISTEN!' very loud, and there was a sudden hush and people turned towards her. This is when I saw it. The hard, cold-eyed, unreadable look she often had on her face.

'Everyone, while we're all still here, I have an important announcement. This is not an easy thing to say, but before things go any further, it is my responsibility to say it. We've all loved welcoming Lola to Pearlbourne and helping her to settle in, and we've all enjoyed this party. It's like she's confirmed her place among us, isn't it?'

There was a ripple of confused clapping but Allegra held up her hand to quieten the room again.

'Well, I have to be honest with you. Lola Nolan-Fitzsimons didn't ever add up to me, not in my head. And while the rest of you have been busy getting taken in, I've been thinking critically, asking questions, keeping my eyes and ears open. Everyone, listen to me.'

Allegra was pointing at me now and her finger was steady and accusatory. I put my hands on the back of Violet's sofa, trying to keep myself steady.

'On the way to this party, I stopped at a supermarket, near here, on Blackrock Main Street.'

The air in the room seemed to swell and then tighten.

'I was picking up a few bits for the party, and a woman at the checkout got chatting. She told me my dress was lovely. She asked me my name and told me hers, Debbie Feely. She asked me where I was going. And when I told her I was going to Lola Nolan Fitzsimon's party in Lavender House, that's when she began to look very confused. Debbie in SuperValu told me that no one is living in Lavender House! She told me that Violet does not have a great-niece. And then I said yes, yes she does and showed her a photo on my phone. A photo of my dorm sister here, Lola.'

Allegra's eyes were set now with crazy delight. She pointed at me. 'This person is not who she says she is. She is not Lola Nolan-Fitzsimons of Lavender House. She is Penny Nolan of Rosemary Flats. She lives next door in a kind of tenement. She has been fooling us and trying to infiltrate our lives and the time has come for the truth to come out.'

'What's going on?' said Miss Lucas, her whole face a shadow of concern.

'I'm telling the truth,' said Allegra, and I looked at her. Angry voices began to rise and people started asking how dare she tell such lies, and was it because she was jealous of me and all sorts of other mean things.

Allegra went on then with more details of the lies she had uncovered. That my family didn't own The Captain's House in Spetses; that I never went to Sharjah International Boarding School. That my mother was a cleaner.

'There's nothing wrong with being a cleaner!' was all I was able to say then.

'You lied though! You said she worked for the government and your dad was in oil.'

'What would you have thought of me if I told you the truth?' I said, knowing now that the game was up.

'What's going on?' said Quin.

'Quiet, everyone,' I said then and all the music had stopped and I pulled a deep warm breath into my lungs as if that would give me strength.

'Allegra is right,' I said. 'She's the one who's telling the truth. I'm the one who's been lying.' And the flames from the fire flashed in Allegra's eyes. I'd been dreading this for so long. I wondered how I'd convinced myself that I was ever going to be able to avoid it.

It was time for me to tell the whole truth now.

To tell everyone who I really was.

In a way it was a relief.

CHAPTER 22

'I am Penny Nolan.'

The place was silent as death then.

'This house belongs to Violet Fitzsimons. And Violet Fitzsimons is not my great-aunt. She gave me a key but I don't live here. I've never lived in this house.'

'This is not your home?' said Miss Lucas, whose face was pale.

'No.'

'Where do you live?' she said, as if she was almost afraid to hear.

'Next door. I live next door.'

'Rosemary Flats?'

'Yes, The Flats.'

'Who do you live with?'

'My mam.'

'And Violet Fitzsimons is no relative of yours?'

'No, no she's not.'

Noise grew again in confused mumblings. Miss Barnard had an expression on her face that I hope I never see on anyone's face ever again.

All the Pearlbourne girls stood in a semi-circle around me and the semi-circle grew as they backed away.

'Lola Nolan-Fitzsimons is an invention!' sneered Allegra. 'She's been trying to fool us all, but I saw through it. It didn't take long to figure it out.'

'I'm sorry,' I said. 'I'm just sorry, to all of you. I never meant this to happen. I've been wanting to tell the truth for ages. I just didn't know how.'

'Well you certainly seem to know how to tell a lot of lies,' said Miss Lucas.

'Yes,' I said.

Jane had come closer and right then, she put her hand on my shoulder and kept it there, and I didn't know what she was trying to say, but it felt for a second like an enormously good thing, an act of friendship. I looked at her and hoped she knew how thankful I was.

'Please go home,' I said to everyone.

'Girls, there is no more time for questions or lingering. We are trespassing illegally on property we should not be in,' announced Miss Lucas. 'Miss Barnard is organising immediate transport and we all must leave straight away. Everyone, gather your things and exit the front door immediately. Form an orderly line, girls.' I could hear the hollowness of Allegra's cold laugh as she grabbed her coat.

And as the other girls melted away, Quin and Jane stood in front of me for another second in a terrible distortion of the way they'd stood in front of me just months before when I'd first arrived at Pearlbourne.

And then all my friends were ushered out into the night by Miss Barnard and it was just Miss Lucas and me, each of us sitting on one of Violet's tapestry chairs by the old phone.

'Talk to me, Lola. What am I to do now?'

'I just want to see my mam. I just want to go home,' I said, 'but I don't even know what to say to her. I don't belong here, and I don't belong in Pearlbourne and I don't belong in my old home, and Miss Lucas, I've become terribly lost, and I am so sorry.'

'I can't leave you here, Lola. I must make sure you get back to your home. I'd like to have a word with your mother, in fact.'

But I begged her not to do that. I blew out all the candles and switched off all the lights and told Miss Lucas that I'd come back tomorrow to make sure the place was left in perfect condition, and together we opened the big Lavender House door and I locked it.

'We can talk again when everything settles down,' said Miss Lucas. 'Now let me see you going into your building so I know you are safely home.'

She walked with me to the battered place where I lived, and I opened the door and pressed one of the light buttons and told her I was sorry again, and it was hard to tell what

Miss Lucas was feeling right then and I was too broken-hearted to wonder.

I sat on the bottom step there in the silence for a while until the timer went off . The darkness was its own relief. I could not face the walk upstairs to Mam who'd ask me about the party and who I'd have to explain everything to.

I called the driver company and said I needed a car, and they said where to and I said the pier in Dún Laoghaire and they said there'd be a driver there in ten and I hoped the driver would be the lovely man who brought me to Pearlbourne but it was not. He drove fast and I was glad to be speeding away. Away from the girls whose school I coveted, away from my two best friends who I'd neglected and forgotten, who I had hurt and baffled, away from my poor mam who'd only ever done her best for me. Away from the huge pretence I'd been trying to pull off. Away from it all.

I walked to the end of the pier and I sat on the cold granite boulder and nine times I tried to ring Violet and nine times there was a weird signal and I tried to think when exactly was the last time we'd spoken. When was the last time I'd got a text from her? I scrolled down to her name and checked. It was weeks ago.

And I thought back to when Violet said goodbye to me at the house and the things she had said. 'I'm going somewhere no one else can go,' was what she had told me. 'This is a thing I have to do on my own.' And I remembered how she'd placed Bluebell in a new home and how final everything had sounded. It had taken me this long to realise what actually must have been going on. Violet was ill, that was it. Violet was dying. She was off on her final journey. That's why she left. It was clear to me now. Maybe she was already dead. The sea was very black and it crashed against the high pier. I'd been so selfish, all focused on my own story, and not really thinking about the person who'd done so much to help me. I'd just used her house to big myself up with people who didn't even know who I was. Violet had been too protective of me to tell me her troubles. And I had been too stupid and greedy to figure them out for myself.

There was a taste of horror and panic in my mouth, like the flash of saliva you get just before you throw up. Everything felt like it was leaning over. Everything was crashing to the ground.

And there was a silence and a blankness in my head.

It felt very cold, but after a short time there came a strange moment of warmth. Another human, right beside me, practically touching me. I looked around. It was Jane. She'd waited outside The Flats. She'd seen the car and me climbing in, and immediately told Miss Lucas, and Miss Lucas had given her permission to follow me. She'd hopped into another taxi and come straight down.

'Oh Jane, I'm so sorry, I'm so sorry about all of this,' I said, and she said nothing, just sat there and put her hand on mine.

'Do you want to talk about it?' she asked eventually.

'I became friends with Violet Fitzsimons,' I began. 'She was the one who first taught me how to play piano. She gave me a lot of money as a gift. I don't have rich parents. I just have my mam. We live in a flat next to Violet's house, and Allegra's right, my mam's a cleaner. She works very hard, but she could never afford to send me to a school like Pearlbourne. Violet Fitzsimons's generosity gave me the opportunity to do that.'

'Wow,' said Jane, but I didn't feel like she hated me. She didn't even sound too shocked.

'And I still have loads and loads of her money left. I'll probably have it for the rest of my life. I've done a lot of frivolous things since she gave it to me. And some of what I did was driven by vanity, or pride, and once by revenge. I had no money, you see, and then suddenly I was rich, and it gave me a feeling I'd never known. For the first time ever, I could do things. I was not powerless.

'I came to Pearlbourne under false pretences. All this time, Jane, I've been pretending to be someone I was not.'

'Listen,' she said, 'I hope you don't mind, but I've told a few other people you're here. They're on their way. One of them's coming now. She's been in touch with Miss Halloran by letter. She knew about the party all along. She was going to surprise you and come home for it but her flight was delayed. I thought you'd like to see her right away.'

And there she was, striding along the pier towards me, dressed in a black evening gown and a jet-black sparkling necklace, looking perfectly healthy, raising long fingers in the air.

And just as she had rescued me once, so it felt she would rescue me again.

'Oh Violet, you're not sick? You're not dead?' I whispered.

'Dear Penny.' She smiled. I introduced her to Jane.

'Why didn't you answer my texts?' I said.

'My blasted mobile phone. Dropped it into the Rio Grande. It's taken me ages to retrieve all my contacts.'

'But Violet, I used your house for a party. I never even asked your permission.'

'I know, and all I can say is good on you! I only wish Rita Halloran had written sooner. I'd have been able to organise some supplies.'

'I'm in terrible trouble.'

'Now, now, what do you mean by that?'

'I pretended Lavender House belonged to me. I told everyone you were my great-aunt.'

'I know, and I rather like the deception, and was not the one responsible for disabusing anyone of it! Now who do I need to speak to, to put the tin hat on the trouble you're in?'

'It's too late. Everything's ruined. I've wrecked the opportunity you gave me.'

Violet said she was sorry too for leaving me when I needed her most and she had lots to tell me about the reasons she'd gone and the secrets of her own that she had kept from me. And I was just delighted she was here.

It was her turn to tell me her own truth.

'As soon as you spoke about the picture you'd found of me and my beloved sister . . . well, it started the chain of events that led me to leaving. Helping you to get to Pearlbourne was part of my waking up, you see. There was another lost girl and that lost girl was my sister and suddenly there was nothing more important than finding her. And for the first time in years, I remembered that it was my fault she'd disappeared.'

'What happened?'

'It was my shame. I'd been hiding it from myself for a long time. It started when I came upon my sister one day in the maths garden all those years ago. It was after prep one summer term and we were allowed to walk the grounds before it got dark. I'd wandered down to the garden which I loved so much and that's when I saw her, sitting on the swing squashed up together with our classmate Louisa. And the thing is, they were kissing. Proper kissing full of love and passion. Those were different days and I was young and though Rosemary made me *promise* on my life and on our sisterhood not to breathe a word of what I had seen to anyone, and though I had vowed I never would, I was, it shames me to say, the architect of her expulsion.

'I roomed with a girl called Cassandra. After lights out, I blurted out the betrayal, telling Cassandra I had seen Louisa and my sister Rose kissing each other on the swing. I told her it was a very important secret and that she must not tell a single soul, but just as I had been treacherously disloyal to my sister, so then Cassandra was disloyal to me. Deep betrayal can be such a casual thing. We can throw the important secrets of others to the wolves in the unplanned blink of an eye. And you see, the news spread and grew and reached the notice of the teachers and then the headmistress, and in those days – well, the world was different and the rules were binding and cruel, and once it was known that they were romantically involved, Rosemary and Louisa were expelled. That was the last time I saw my twin. Her departure was hurried, her exile complete. I could not speak of it for all these years. Instead, I buried the unhappy truth and my culpability in it – I wrapped it in soft, happy stories of perfection. I could not bear to talk of it to anyone. I could not admit it to you, that I – the woman you so looked up to – had once ratted her sister out with such terrible consequences.

'I papered over the great cracks of my guilt, you see, by only allowing myself to remember happiness at Pearlbourne – I collected only the lovely moments in my head the way you might pick pretty shells from a littered beach. And all the time I could not bear to remember the sadness of my sister and the miserable time she had to endure, and the way she was demonised and rejected. I could not let myself accept the role I had played in her expulsion from our school and her exile from her home, and all the bad things that happened as a result – the selling of Rosemary House and its awful decline, and the environment that you have had to grow up in. Mea culpa. All my fault, it turns out, my dear.'

Jane and I sat either side of her on that rock at the end of the pier. She took my right hand and Jane's left, joined up like the links of a chain.

'But I've faced it head-on now. And telling you is part of the making of amends as indeed, there is much to make amends for.

'Louisa and Rosemary changed their names and started a new life in Mexico. Why Mexico? I still have no idea, but I've been there, and they've made such a lovely home. In those days here in Ireland Rosemary would not have been allowed to be who she was. Turns out Mexico was no different but they were from a far-off place and not subjected to the rules that others had to comply with. It's hard to explain to modern girls like you. Rosemary simply would not have it because if anyone was going to live her truth then it was my sister, and so was Louisa.

'Turns out the joke's on the rest of the world because they are married now, and happier than anyone I know. And all these years I've tried to put away the thoughts of what terrible wilderness Rosemary was enduring when all the time she's the one who's been insisting on this happy life, and it was me, Penny, me who was in a wilderness I'd created for myself. It was you, my dear darling girl, who opened the door to something better. It was you who made up my mind. Connection with people is more important than anything.

'I had to go to find her. I couldn't waste any more time. We are connected again, and Rosemary and Louisa are home at last! There is so much to make up for, but it's not too late.'

There was a noise then. I thought it might be thunder, and I looked to the sky to see if rain was coming, but though the night was very cold, the stars were pinpricks of brightness above and the wind was soft. The sound was from something else.

'There you are!' came a shout from behind and we turned again. It was Matt and Kitty trundling towards us on their skateboards and Mam in her coat, quite a way behind, hurrying to reach me.

And soon I was surrounded by them too. They should have been angrier with me than anyone – they had a right to be – but they are my friends and Mam is my family, and they knew I was in trouble, and they showed me nothing but friendship and love. I introduced Jane and Violet to everyone. And the goodness that surrounded me felt like a solid thing. For a moment I thought it might knock me over.

'Why are you so kind to me? Why did you help me as much as you did?' I asked Violet. 'Why did you give me all that money? I didn't deserve it. I'm an awful person. I've told so many lies just so I could feel more important than I did. People needed the money more than I did but I kept most of it for myself.'

Violet's eyes filled with tears.

'You are not an awful person. There is no malice within a hundred miles of you. You're not guilty of anything apart from wishing the world was different than it is. You may have made mistakes, but it doesn't make you a bad person. Bad rumours used to be spread about me – untrue stories about me being some kind of monster. It doesn't matter whether you are Lola Nolan-Fitzsimons, or Penny Nolan. You befriended me without motive or guile, and your doing that banished those horrid stories, and made an extraordinary difference in my life.'

'Also, lovey, you fixed our building in dangerous need of repair,' said Mam.

'There was black mould,' Kitty explained, 'all over the walls of The Flats, and Penny was the one who hired the builders to have it seen to.'

'Yeah,' said Matt. 'She tried to tell us it was Michael Graves but he never would have done anything like that. We always knew it had something to do with her.'

'She bought gifts for her family and friends,' added Kitty, 'including Frisbee golf. And she arranged the best holiday anyone has ever been on.'

'See?' said Violet. 'Think about that! All the good things

you've already done with the money that otherwise would have just sat there in an old woman's bank account. And furthermore,' she added, 'I have it on good authority that you enriched Pearlbourne Academy in many important ways. If you're looking for the truth, the truth is you are a lovely, clever, talented girl. Who else in the world do you know who could do what you have done: start in a strange new school, learn to ride a horse, get such good grades and best of all, in less than a semester, learn to play Beethoven's Pathétique? You were kind to me when no one else was. You liked me despite what people said. You and I shared the same interests, and we loved the same music and those things became the bridge across which a special connection has been made. I saw you tolerate difficult conditions with great fortitude. I knew of your longing for a good education and of your unhappiness. I took the time to listen to you only in the same way you took the time to listen to me. You cared for Bluebell, saving her from coming to an unpleasant end. You fetched my groceries and polished my silver. You paid attention and gave regard to the stories of when I was a girl and in this way you returned memories to me . . . memories I thought I had lost.'

There were more tears then and there was more hugging and the *ding ding ding* of the yachts moored in the harbour and we might have stayed there all night until Violet announced:

'Right, may I say everyone, this is getting rather

ridiculous. It's the middle of a January night. I'm barely off the plane. Come on, back to my house this minute! I expect you could all do with a hot drink and a warm up.'

We stayed up all night at Violet's who, despite saying she was shattered from exhaustion, insisted on making toast. Matt told me I never needed to pretend. He said as far as he was concerned, the real me was a thousand times more brilliant and interesting than any new version I could have invented. He held out his hand to me and I held mine out to him and we were holding hands then and I knew something I'd never known before and I looked at the shape of his fingers and he leaned towards me and if Kitty and Jane and Mam and Violet hadn't come in from the kitchen with the tea and toast right at that moment, I'm pretty sure I would have kissed him.

In the days that followed I met Rosemary and Louisa too. Rosemary looked exactly the same as Violet except her skin was tanned and she wore fabulous big boots. I told them I could never go back to Pearlbourne, not after everything. All three of the old Pearlbournians disagreed.

'You absolutely must return. I shall speak to Lucina Lucas,' said Violet.

'But the important thing is to return as you, not as someone you were pretending to be,' said Rosemary. 'That shall be your mission.'

'There will be disapproval and sneering at first, no doubt,' added Louisa, and a ripple of dread shuddered through me at the thought of what the Pearlbourne girls would say to me if I ever rocked up at their domed doorway again. 'None of it will matter, for you have been through the worst of the punishment already. No amount of scorn from others will come close to the cruelty you have already inflicted on yourself.'

'It was a terrible set of lies, OK, but I told them because I was trying to protect myself,' I said, still trying to make sense of what I'd done and why.

'By denying who you really are?' asked Rosemary. 'That, my dear, is not self-protection, that's self-annihilation. There isn't a single girl in Pearlbourne, not even the meanest of them, who could possibly have held you in the same contempt in which you have held yourself.'

'Precisely!' added Violet. 'And in any case, the girls who sneer about this, will sneer no matter what. You might as well learn to withstand it. Good practice for life, I say. And if you power through, you'll find people there who'll take you as you are, and will admire you for having had the courage to declare your right to be Penny Nolan. You won't be doing it just for yourself. You'll be doing it for every girl who ever hid behind some pretend version of herself.'

And just then Rosemary reached for Louisa's hand, and held it, and we all sat in a warm silence thinking quietly about the price those women had paid long ago simply for insisting on being who they were.

'Finish it out. Don't turn back now. Keep facing towards the thing you want so much. Just sort out the good stuff from the bad,' Violet said.

'What do you think?' I asked Matt and he said he reckoned it made sense. 'Just promise me one thing. Don't start talking like Allegra.'

I promised I definitely wouldn't.

'And don't start calling your mam "Mummy",' added Kitty and I said I'd never do that either.

'If you go back, it will give you a chance to miss me,' said Matt.

'I've missed you already.'

'Glad to hear it!' he said and his dimples, I realised right then, were gorgeous. Just like the rest of him.

I spent some brilliant January days with my friends and everyone in Rosemary Flats. I told Mam the whole story about the money and she wasn't even annoyed. She was delighted. We went on a massive shopping spree. She has a new car now, and we've done up the flat and unstuck the kitchen window and she's given up smoking, and she doesn't know herself. I told her she should give up the cleaning job too but she says she likes her work. There's great satisfaction in it, and it's even nicer now that she has a reliable form of transport and no financial pressure.

Kitty's mam is seeing a therapist now, working on her

anger issues, and Bluebell is back in Lavender House, which is another thing that makes me feel the world has rebalanced itself again.

I did go back to Pearlbourne. I'm still here. In fourth year now. Miss Engels said I should write it all down – make sense of the crazy things that happened, but I don't think I'll ever make total sense of it, to be honest. Writing is good though. Putting it on the page helps me to get the measure of myself and of the decisions I made and of why I made them. When I can, I often come out here to the maths garden and sit on the measuring swing. Restoring the garden has been the best activity ever – a project I proposed when I came back. With help from the Pearlbourne Foundation and under Daly's enthusiastic (if sometimes authoritarian) supervision it became the stayovers' weekend project. We started in September. I can't believe how quickly the place has changed. It's almost finished now, and it's looking great. But there's still some work to do to get it perfect in time for Violet, Louisa and Rosemary. They've been invited to make an official visit at the end of the year, to celebrate their connection with the school and to make sure that Louisa and Rosemary's names finally get engraved on the wall of girls.

It really is magical here in the Pearlbourne forest – all November oranges and browns and leaves whipping around in whirls. Actually, I'd better get going because the bell will ring soon and I've got poetry with Miss Engels who cannot bear it when people are late.

There've been other changes here since last year. Miss Lucas gave a big assembly speech before I came back. Jane told me about it, word for word. Lucas said that everyone had a lot of reflecting to do. She said they all – the teachers and the students – had to think very hard about the reasons why a perfectly nice and talented child felt she had to go to so much trouble to cover up her true identity. She claimed this said much more about the flaws in Pearlbourne than it did about the flaws in me. They're working on a proper scholarship programme now. I'm on the committee.

Mam has been on a visit to Pearlbourne and so have Tony and Breda and Kitty and Matt. Winter concert was held in November this year, and they had front row seats. Afterwards parents and friends came to the ref for nibbles. I was a bit worried about how my Rosemary Flats Crew would fit in with the fragrant mothers and sharp-suited fathers, but everyone got on brilliantly. I was proud because my friends and family are decent and generous and lovely, no matter who they're talking to. Not all the girls in Pearlbourne have people like that in their lives. The only hiccup of the evening was me having to tell Allegra to stop flirting with Matt. 'Back off,' is what I said to her. 'He's taken.'

Mostly people have stopped talking about the drama of

last year and the big reveal at the party in Lavender House. Allegra had a party the following term and loads of boys showed up and two of them took the keys of her father's Maserati and crashed it into a lamppost – so that's what everyone's talking about these days. Next term I'm sure it will be something else.

It would be wrong of me to say there aren't brilliant things about Pearlbourne because there are many, but it's not the paradise I once dreamed it would be. There are unhappy people here too. They hide it well. They cry in the dark, or fight silently with their families on the privacy of their mobiles, or try to contact their parents who often take ages to answer back. Allegra Queensbury has been in boarding school since she was eight. And in general, I'm not sure if it's healthy to have an automatic jumping reflex response to the sound of a ringing bell.

I once imagined I was going to a perfect place but what I found was something else. A place full of history and tradition? Yeah, that's true. A place with girls from privileged families? Sure. But perfect paradise? Definitely not. Not even close.

I'm not saying money doesn't help. It helps a massive amount. It makes opportunities and provides comforts and takes away millions of tiny moments of worry and fear. But it doesn't make you feel good about yourself. If you don't feel that in the core of you, then all the money in the world is not going to do it for you.

There is something else that makes me better on the inside, something that floods through me like a wave, past the rocky coastline of my anger and my sorrows and all the things I am still afraid of. Something that makes the world stand still, filling the dark spaces in me with light: of all the brilliant gifts that Violet gave me, music will always be the greatest, and I will keep on thanking her for it – because of the thousand times it has saved me. And because it saves me still.

And now I have to run or I'll definitely be late for class – and Miss Engels will lose her sense of reason.

ACKNOWLEDGEMENTS

I am hugely grateful to the musicians and teachers who answered my long list of questions with such patience and kindness. Thank you, Mary Scarlett, Fí Scarlett, Robert S J Lucas, Anne Cunningham and Caoimhe Ní Riain. Any remaining errors of accuracy or precision are mine alone.

My brilliant friends and colleagues at the University of Limerick are too numerous to name but I take the liberty of being specific when it comes to Sarah MacCurtain, Eoin Reeves, Tina O'Toole, Carrie Griffin, Aelish Nagle, Michael Griffin, Meg Harper, Rob Doyle, Gavin McCrea, Joseph O'Connor and Donal Ryan.

My friends at Writepace continue to be constant sources of inspiration to me: Noel Harrington, Sheila Killian, Dan Mooney, Kerry Neville, Bob Burke, Hilda McHugh, Jo Gibney, Geri Maye, Sue Loughnane, Jackie O'Shaughnessy, Vivienne McKechnie and Cat Hogan. Thanks also to the support and friendship of writers Kit De Waal, Louise O'Neill, Marian Keyes and Justine Carbery.

Elaina Ryan of CBI, Siobhan Tierney of Hachette Ireland and Collette Cotter of O'Mahony's bookshop have been kind supporters of my books and my writing for a long time now, as have all the students of the UL MA in Creative Writing and UL Creative Writing Winter School.

In 2019, Offaly County Council awarded me the Birr writers' residency at Brendan House where I wrote a significant chunk of this novel. Thanks to my hostess Rosalind Fanning.

Much love and thanks to Jo Unwin for everything she has always done to support my creative work; to Helen Thomas for her kind, wise, tender editorial heart; and to Rachel Boden, Sarah Lambert, Dominic Kingston, Flic Highet and all at Hachette for the amazing professionalism in helping this book to take shape. Also massive thanks to Michelle Brackenborough for the wonderful cover.

To Melanie Sheridan, my best friend and first reader par excellence; to Gráinne O'Brien and Eoin Devereux whose belief in the creative process is a kind of magic; and to the mighty clans of O'Dea and Fitzgerald.

Love to my brilliant, kind, lovely family: Ben, David, Morgan, Alma, Paul, Meredith, Aoife, Elizabeth, Eoghan, Stef and Gabbie. And once more and forever, to Ger.

MORE BRILLIANT BOOKS

BY
SARAH MOORE FITZGERALD